'Was it necessary to slap me first?'

'Technically no, spiritually yes,' Polly replied, dropping the syringe into the sharps bin. 'Right, let's get you sewn up, *Dr* Gregory.'

Matt rolled on to his stomach, propped his chin on his folded hands and mumbled something.

'What?'

'I said I'm sorry. I should have told you who I was but I was enjoying your ministrations. . .'

Caroline Anderson's nursing career was brought to an abrupt halt by a back injury, but her interest in medical things led her to work first as a medical secretary, and then, after completing her teacher training, as a lecturer in Medical Office Practice to trainee medical secretaries. In addition to writing, she also runs her own business from her home in rural Suffolk, where she lives with her husband, two daughters, mother and dog.

Previous Titles

PRACTICE MAKES PERFECT
RELATIVE ETHICS

For John, who is definitely husband material.

SAVING
DR GREGORY

BY
CAROLINE ANDERSON

MILLS & BOON LIMITED
ETON HOUSE   18–24 PARADISE ROAD
RICHMOND   SURREY   TW9 1SR

*First published in Great Britain 1992
by Mills & Boon Limited*

© Caroline Anderson 1992

*Australian copyright 1992
Philippine copyright 1992
This edition 1992*

ISBN 0 263 77629 8

*Set in 10½ on 12 pt Linotron Times
03-9204-50190
Typeset in Great Britain by Centracet, Cambridge
Made and printed in Great Britain*

CHAPTER ONE

IT WAS Polly's favourite time of day, and she curled up on the window-seat overlooking the valley and cuddled her steaming mug of coffee. Her breath was misting on the window, and she scrubbed at it with her sleeve. It was cold in the sitting-room in the mornings, but the view was so spectacular that she didn't mind.

The little window was set in the thickness of the cob walls, and the seat tucked into the little nook was fast becoming Polly's favourite place. Admittedly it wasn't very comfortable, but the view was something else. In front of the tiny rented cottage ran a narrow, winding lane, hedged with hawthorn and dog-rose, with occasional wild cherries standing like sentinels along the route.

Beyond the lane was a field, dipping away into the distance, with neat lines of plough showing tiny tips of green as the winter wheat broke the surface of the soil. Beyond that, a river wound lazily along the valley floor before the land rose steeply on the other side in a heavily wooded slope. As it rose, the willows and poplars gave way to other trees, beech and oak and sycamore, with the occasional white trunk of a silver birch gleaming in the distance. The autumn colours in the old wood were at their best on this early November day, and the morning sun slanting low across the hill behind her caught the leaves and turned them to flame.

It was an isolated spot, but that didn't worry Polly. She wasn't afraid of her own company, and she wasn't afraid of her fellow man, either. In her experience the vast majority of people were good and decent, and the media's exaggeration had led a great many people to believe otherwise. Polly thought it was a tremendous shame.

Take this man, for instance, she mused. He jogged along the lane every morning—at least he had in the week Polly had been living here. Anybody could see that he was harmless, for all that he was big. He just looked reliable, honest and solid and trustworthy. It didn't occur to Polly that she was being fanciful, or that she was making judgements based on speculation and not fact. She just knew, without any question, that she could trust him with her life.

He was earlier today, she thought. Last week it had been about eight-fifteen, and she had even passed him one morning in her car on the way to work.

Today it was barely half-past seven, and Polly was only up and dressed because she wanted to get to work early to sort out her surgery shelves and rearrange her supplies before the clinics started.

The man drew level with her cottage, jogging steadily across from left to right. The sun was shining on his back, highlighting the breadth of his shoulders and the glint of gold in his neat brown hair. The boy-next-door grown up, Polly thought, and smiled to herself as she watched him.

There was a car coming towards him now, and

Polly frowned as she saw it bearing down on him with no attempt to reduce speed. She saw a greasy sheen on the windscreen, and realised in horror that the driver was momentarily blinded by the sun.

She heard the man shout, and at the last second the car swerved, sliding out of control on the wet leaves that covered the lane. With the car headed straight for him, the man threw himself out of its path, crashing into the hedge as the car slewed past him and ground into the bank on the other side.

Polly didn't hesitate. Grabbing her coat off the peg by the door, she ran out into the lane and towards the jogger. He was picking himself up by the time she got there, and looked at her in surprise.

'Are you all right?' she asked anxiously.

'Yes, I'm fine. How about the people in the car?'

'I'll check them.' She turned on her heel and ran over to the car just as the passenger door opened and the driver struggled out.

'Sorry, mate!' he called. 'Didn't see you—damn sun got in my eyes. You OK?'

'Fine,' he repeated. 'What about you?'

His voice was warm and deep, Polly noted with detachment. Just what she would have expected. The jogger had every right to be angry, having nearly been mown down. Many people would have been, she thought, but his first concern had been for the occupants of the car; that just reinforced her opinion of him.

Now they were shaking hands, and the driver was returning to his car and pulling away, considerably more slowly than before. She turned back to the jogger.

'Are you sure you're all right?'

He nodded. 'Just a bit shaken up. I'll be OK.' He frowned at the lane. 'Where did you spring from?'

'The cottage. I'm renting it. I'd better get on, if you're sure——?'

He grinned. 'Fine—see?' He turned to jog away from her, and his left leg collapsed under him. Making a grab for Polly, he swore softly under his breath and bent to explore his left calf.

His right hand was gripping her shoulder firmly, and Polly tucked her left arm around his waist to support him. He felt lean and solid, without an ounce of fat. He was also shaking slightly, probably with shock.

'What's the problem?'

He shook his head and straightened, frowning at his left hand. It was streaked with blood and he glanced down at his leg again.

'Don't know. It hurts, though. It didn't a minute ago.'

'That often happens,' Polly hastened to reassure him. 'Often we don't feel an injury until it's safe to do so. I suppose it's a safety mechanism. Let's get you inside and have a closer look.'

Still supporting him around his waist, she changed sides so that his injured leg was next to her and she could give him better support, and they made their way slowly into the cottage. The top of her head came up to his chin, and his arm rested comfortably across her shoulders. They fitted well together, she thought idly.

Once in the kitchen, he sank gratefully on to a chair and flexed his leg.

'It feels as if there's something in it,' he muttered, and Polly stripped off her coat, turned on the kettle and washed her hands thoroughly.

'Take off your tracksuit bottoms,' she instructed, rummaging in the kitchen cupboard for her first-aid kit.

'Do you say that to all the strange men you meet?' he asked, laughter brimming in his voice.

'Only the ones who fall in my hedge and write themselves off,' she returned. 'You're quite safe, I'm a qualified nurse. I'm also going to be late for work, so if you could co-operate, please?' When she turned back he had pulled his trousers off and was standing on one leg in his jogging shorts, craning his neck to see the back of his calf.

'Here,' she said, and grasping his ankle firmly, she lifted his well-muscled but lacerated lower leg and propped it across the seat of the chair. 'Stand still. You don't need to see, I do,' she told him frankly, and then examined the area without touching it for a few seconds. Because he had been exercising, the blood vessels were all dilated and so the scratches were bleeding freely. However, there only seemed to be one serious wound.

'What's wrong?' he asked, peering over his shoulder again.

'Stop squirming around,' she chided. 'You've got hawthorns in it, and a nasty cut. I'll clean it up and lift out the thorns with tweezers, but you really ought to have stitches in the cut, I think. You'll have to keep still.'

'Yes, Nurse,' he said in a mock-submissive voice, and Polly's mouth twitched into a smile.

She cleaned the area as gently as possible, and then after warning him, swabbed the cuts with antiseptic.

He winced and his leg muscles clenched involuntarily. Polly apologised and carried on swabbing. 'It could have been worse,' she told him, 'you might have sat in the hedge.'

His choked laugh was cut off abruptly when she swabbed him again.

'You haven't asked if I've got AIDS,' he said through gritted teeth, and Polly straightened for a second and looked him dead in the eye.

'I should think not! I would imagine, as you're an intelligent person, that you would have had the grace to tell me. You're far more likely to have Hepatitis B——'

'Sorry, all clear. I've had my jabs.'

'Tetanus?' she asked.

He shook his head. 'Not recently.'

'Well, you must. Go to the doctor today and have a booster.' She bent her head over his leg again. 'You don't know what you could have picked up from these thorns. Infected animals could have brushed against them or anything.'

'Unlikely,' he murmured, watching with interest as she removed the tweezers from the cup of boiling water and dipped them in the antiseptic to cool them. 'I'm probably in more danger from those things.'

'That's the most sterile I can get them at this sort of notice. Sorry,' she added as he flinched again. 'You look as if you've had a run-in with a porcupine. There,' she laid the tweezers aside and swabbed the cut again, then wiped it dry. 'I'll put a butterfly plaster on it for now, but I really would recommend that you go to your doctor.'

Polly pressed the plaster in place, covering it with a sterile gauze dressing, and stood back to admire her handiwork. 'You'll do. I must get on. Can I give you a lift home?'

'Please, if you've got time. Are you going through Longridge?'

'I work there. That's no trouble.'

She picked up her coat, and handed him his tracksuit bottoms. 'I'm afraid they're ruined,' she said apologetically.

He shrugged. 'They were ancient anyway.' He hobbled out to the car, commenting as he went that his leg felt much better without the thorns.

She drove carefully into town, following his directions and dropping him in front of a lovely cottage, set back from the road behind a low wall in a quiet little lane just off the town centre.

'Take care, now, and do go to the doctors' with that. I'm sure they'd rather see you *before* it goes septic,' she said cheerfully.

'I don't doubt it,' he said with a laugh, leaning down through the passenger door to throw her a cheeky grin. 'Thank you. . .?'

'Polly,' she supplied.

'Thank you, Polly. You're a gem.'

She blushed. 'Rubbish. I'll see you,' she mumbled.

The grin widened. 'Yes, you will. Go carefully, Pollyanna.'

She pulled away, and glancing back in her rear-view mirror, she saw him give a jaunty wave before turning to hobble into his house. Nice man, she thought, even if he did call her Pollyanna. She wondered what his name was, and if she *would* see him again. . .

Polly arrived at the surgery in good time for her first clinic, but not in time to turn out her shelves. Oh, well, there was always the evening. She could stay late—goodness knew, there was precious little else for her to do as she didn't know anybody yet.

She hung her coat in the little cloakroom and studied herself in the mirror for a moment. There was a liveliness in her gentle brown eyes that hadn't been there earlier this morning, and a soft touch of colour on her cheekbones, the remains of the blush put there by her intriguing encounter. With a little smile, she tidied her lively nut-brown curls and added a dash of soft pink lipstick before going into Reception.

'Morning, Angela, morning, Sue,' she said cheerfully. 'Anything exciting I should know about?'

'Other than that Dr Gregory is back today? Not really,' Angela told her. 'Here's your surgery list—they're mainly inoculations and routine dressings. Mrs Major's in for a diabetic check, and there are one or two to have stitches out. That's this morning, then this afternoon you're working with Dr Gregory on the ante-natal clinic. He'll talk to you about that when he comes in. Sue's got your notes out for this morning. Here,' Angela handed her a pile of patients' envelopes, and headed for the door.

'Dr Haynes wants to dictate some letters before surgery starts. Must fly. Help yourself to coffee.'

The practice manager-cum-medical secretary ran lightly up the stairs to the senior partner's surgery, and left Polly sorting through the notes. Sue, the receptionist, was on the phone, and Polly was alone when the surgery door was pushed open and her jogger limped in and came round to the door into Reception.

'Hello again,' he said, his warm toffee voice touched with humour. He was wearing a light grey suit and tortoiseshell specs, and looked even more like the boy next door.

What a nice smile, Polly thought, and returned it with interest. 'Hello. I'm glad you decided to take my advice. If you can hang on a minute, I'll see who can fit you in.'

'Actually, it's you I wanted to see——'

'Oh, no,' Polly replied, 'you really ought to be seen by a doctor——'

His lips twitched. 'Nonsense. All I need is a tetanus booster, as you so thoughtfully pointed out when you were tactfully trying to discover if I had AIDS——'

'I did no such thing! You brought that up! I would never dream——'

'You should, Pollyanna. You can't be too careful.'

Polly pretended to scowl at him. 'Don't be absurd. Look at you! Unless you've had a contaminated blood transfusion——'

'I could be a haemophiliac.'

Polly shook her head firmly. 'No. I've seen your legs. No haemophiliac has knees like that, with straight, strong joints—and anyway, you would have bled to death on my kitchen floor.'

'There could be worse fates,' he joked.

'Not for my kitchen floor!' Polly replied laughingly. 'Now come on, out of here, please. If you go round to the window I'll get the receptionist to make you an appointment with one of the doctors. Who do you usually see?'

'I have more to do with Gregory than the others,' he replied, still lounging in the doorway, an engaging smile playing around his nicely sculptured lips, his blue eyes behind his tortoiseshell specs twinkling merrily.

Polly was at a loss. How could she get him out of the reception area into the waiting-room? Short of picking him up—and he was much too big for that? probably a shade under six feet, but she knew from her contact with him that morning that every inch of him was solid bone and muscle, and at five feet three in her shoes she didn't stand a snow-flake's. . .sighing, she turned away to the desk.

'I'm sorry,' she said over her shoulder, 'but Dr Gregory has been away on holiday and he's rather booked up this morning.'

'But I only want to see you, Pollyanna——'

'The name's Nurse Barnes, and please don't call me Pollyanna,' she almost snapped, turning round as she did so to find that her nose was in line with the middle of his tie, and so close that she could see the fine silk weave. She swallowed.

'Patients really aren't allowed in here. Please go into the waiting area, Mr—er. . .'

'Ah, Polly, I see you've met Dr Gregory. Good,

good.' The senior partner swept in, clapped Polly's intruder on the back and grinned at them both. 'Good to have you back, old chap. Matt, this is our new nurse, Polly Barnes. She's a real breath of spring.'

He smiled apologetically. 'I know. She has the hands of an angel, as well.' He laughed at Dr Haynes' puzzled frown. 'I fell in her hedge this morning, and she tended me, very sympathetically.'

Polly felt the heat rising from her toes—whether from her own humiliation or from his praise, she wasn't sure. Scarlet, she muttered something about having to get on and excused herself hastily.

'I'll see you later for that tetanus jab, Polly,' Matt called after her.

Polly smiled grimly. That could be a mistake. The way she was feeling, it could provide her with a wonderful means of revenge! 'You do that,' she called back, and stomped into her little room, mortified. He could have said something—anything! Rat. Low-down, sneaky, devious rat! So much for trusting him!

She was giving vent to her feelings when he stuck his head round the door and grinned. 'Your notes,' he said, and limped off down the corridor, whistling jauntily.

Polly wondered if he realised how close he was to having a hypodermic in the back of his neck.

The day was the usual hectic scrabble, with a mish-mash of inoculations interwoven with various other routine checks, like Mrs Major, the young diabetic who was having her three-monthly check-up.

Polly weighed her, took her blood pressure and a blood sample for the hypotest. 'Your blood sugar's a little on the low side, Mrs Major,' Polly told her.

'Oh, I'm not surprised. I couldn't eat this morning—I tried, but—to tell you the truth, I've been off my food for a couple of days.'

Polly frowned. 'I'll get you a cup of tea and a biscuit in a minute. Your blood pressure's down a bit, too. I don't suppose you could be pregnant?'

Mrs Major laughed. 'Oh, no, Nurse. No chance. We're always very careful—we don't want a family yet, and James always—no, I couldn't be.'

Polly persisted. 'When is your next period due?'

The woman shrugged. 'Any time now, I think. Why? You don't seriously think I could be pregnant, do you? I'm sure—although, come to think of it——'

She flushed.

'Yes?' Polly prompted gently.

'There might have been one occasion—but surely. . .?'

Polly smiled. 'It only takes once, Mrs Major. Let me see if your doctor can fit you in now, just to be on the safe side. Who is your GP?'

'Dr Gregory,' she replied, and Polly almost ground her teeth in frustration.

'Fine,' she said with a forced smile, and asking Mrs Major to hang on, she went along the corridor to Dr Gregory's room and tapped on the door, popping her head round.

He had an elderly man with him whom Polly had seen the previous week to dress an ulcer on his leg, and she smiled at him in genuine pleasure. 'Hello, Mr Grey. How are you doing?' she asked warmly.

'Oh, not so bad, my dear. I'll be along to see you directly,' he told her with a twinkle.

'Jolly good. I'll look forward to it——'

'Did you want something, Nurse Barnes, or is this merely a social call?' Matt asked a trifle abruptly, and Polly straightened up like a naughty girl.

'I've got a lady I'd like you to have a look at when you've got a minute, Dr Gregory.'

'Fine. Hang on to her; Mr Grey and I have almost finished, I think.'

'Fine,' Polly gulped and shot out of his room, pulling the door to behind herself and sagging against it with a sigh. Why did he always seem to catch her at a disadvantage?

She went back into her little surgery, and continued with Mrs Major's check-up, examining her eyes and feet for any sign of the deterioration that diabetes could cause. Everything was fine, except that she was beginning to feel a little nauseated and was probably going to go into a hypo if she didn't have something to eat soon.

Polly gave her a glucose tablet, and went to find some biscuits from the kitchen. When she got back, Dr Gregory was in her chair, holding Mrs Major's hands and talking soothingly to her.

'She's going into a hypo, Polly. I'll have to give her some IV dextrose, I think. What's her blood sugar?'

'One point five.'

'I wonder if we can get it up with food?' Matt suggested, eyeing the biscuits, but Mrs Major by now was beyond co-operating. 'Polly, could you draw me up ten mls of twenty-per-cent dextrose?' he asked over his shoulder, then, scooping the nearly comatose woman up in his arms, he laid her gently on the couch and rolled up her sleeve; putting a tourniquet around her upper arm, he started looking for a vein.

'Can't find one. They're all contracted down—ah, here's one.' Taking the syringe from Polly, he inserted the needle, pulled back to check the positioning in the vein and then flicking off the tourniquet, slowly injected the glucose solution.

The effect was remarkable. Mrs Major groaned and rolled on to her side, complaining of nausea, and Polly grabbed a kidney dish and pushed it under her chin in the nick of time.

'Well done, Pollyanna,' Matt murmured, withdrawing the needle and dropping the used syringe into the yellow sharps bin. Mrs Major was groaning, and Matt laid his hand over the vein and pressed firmly.

'Hello, there. How are you feeling?'

She attempted a smile. 'Awful. I have been for days. I think maybe Nurse Barnes is right.'

Matt raised an eyebrow at Polly.

'There is some possibility that Mrs Major is pregnant,' Polly explained quietly. 'Her blood pressure's lower than usual, and she's been nauseated in the mornings.'

Matt nodded. 'Let's just have a look at you, Mrs Major,' he suggested, and helped her undo her skirt and slide it down to her hips. He checked her eyes and throat, the glands in her neck and under her arms, and listened to her chest before moving down to palpate her abdomen gently. 'When did your last period start?' he asked.

'I've been trying to think. The day we finished putting in the central heating,' she decided. 'That was the end of September—twenty-seventh, something like that?'

Polly picked up a calendar. 'That makes you ten days overdue, Mrs Major.'

'Oh,' she said, subdued.

'Oh, Matt echoed. 'Would it be bad news?'

She shook her head. 'Not really—although I don't know what James will say.'

Matt smiled. 'If it's simply a case of accelerating your plunge into parenthood, he'll probably get used to it very quickly. If not, well, he'll come round, I'm sure. I'm much more concerned about your physical well-being at the moment. Certainly there's nothing else obviously wrong with you. Is your diabetes normally well controlled?'

'Yes—well, it has been. It's only recently that I've been feeling off-colour, but I really have tried to eat.'

'You must—I know that sounds impossibly trite, but you know the importance of maintaining your intake of carbohydrates. Try eating crackers and drinking cold water with ice in it. Slices of apple are supposed to be very good, too. Get James to wait on you a bit.' He grinned. 'Do him good. Men have it far too easy during pregnancy—always assuming that's what's wrong with you! I suppose it wouldn't be a bad idea to take a sample of urine and run a pregnancy test, Polly. Can you sort that out?'

Polly nodded. 'Of course. Do you want Mrs Major to come back this afternoon if it's positive?'

Matt shook his head. 'I don't think there's any need. If you find you can't eat, then we can arrange for you to go into hospital so that you can be consistently monitored and maintained. Hopefully it won't come to that—I don't think it will—but they may want to take over your ante-natal care.'

'Aren't there any pills you can give me?'

'I'd rather not,' he said, after a slight pause. 'I'm never sure about them. Let's give it a whirl without first. I'm sure you'll be all right.'

He rose to his feet and limped to the door.

'Oh!' Mrs Major exclaimed 'You've hurt yourself!'

He gave her a lopsided grin. 'Polly beat me up,' he said sorrowfully.

'Ignore him,' Polly advised, throwing him a black look and fighting down another blush.

He limped off down the corridor, chuckling quietly. Polly explained to the bemused patient that Matt had nearly been run off the road that morning.

'Lucky for him you were there!' Mrs Major said, and Polly smiled tightly. She was not a vindictive person, but this tetanus injection was beginning to sound attractive!

It was much later that Polly got her revenge, and it wasn't at all as she had expected. She met up with Matt over lunch—a snack taken in Reception after he came back from doing house calls, while he explained what he wanted her to do during the ante-natal clinics. First she was to weigh each patient and take her blood pressure, then check her urine with the Multistix, entering the results on the co-op card as well as the patient's notes. Then Matt wanted her present to chaperon during examinations, but not otherwise. There were six patients booked for the afternoon session, and he ran over the notes quickly with Polly. There was nothing unusual about any of them, except for one elderly primip, a thirty-five-year-old unmarried woman who had decided she wanted a child.

'She shouldn't be a problem,' Matt said, 'she's very fit and healthy. She's in a stable relationship but there's no question of marriage, so don't ask her, and for goodness' sake don't call her Mrs Harding. It's Ms—on pain of death! On the other hand, this very married lady——' he thrust some notes at Polly '—Sarah Goddard, has three children already. The last one was born in the car on the way to hospital, and she only just got there with the second. Going on her record, we've opted for a home delivery! She's due at the beginning of January, but she probably won't go to term. Right, I've got some letters to write and some results to sift through. I'll see you at three on the dot. We've only got an hour, so we have to keep moving fairly rapidly. If anyone has a problem, we tend to run over and lose our tea break. I really don't want to, especially as I'm on call tonight, but that's the way the cookie crumbles.'

He gave a wry smile, and Polly felt herself respond against her better judgement. He was such a tease, she thought, but such a nice person with it. She watched as he unfolded himself and limped cautiously towards the door.

'Have you done anything about that leg yet?' she asked, concerned despite herself.

He shook his head. 'I can't reach it to stitch it, but I think you're right. I don't suppose you'd like to do it now—that is, if I can trust you?'

Polly's eyes widened. 'Me?' she mouthed.

'You can suture, can't you?'

She nodded. 'Yes, but——'

'But nothing. Please? Stephen and Mike are too busy, and I hate to see a good woman go to waste——'

Polly stood up and stalked past him. 'Come on, then,' she threw over her shoulder, and went into his consulting room.

'Take your trousers off and lie down,' she instructed, scrubbing up her hands and sorting out the lignocaine injection and the tetanus booster.

'I get a feeling of *déjà vu*,' he commented, kicking off his shoes and removing his trousers.

'Just shut up and lie down,' she said irritably. She didn't like the way he made her feel, not one bit. She was never irritable—never. He brought out a side of her she didn't even know existed, and it was a side she didn't think she liked. However, he seemed to hit all the wrong buttons all the time.

She picked up the lignocaine syringe and got Matt to check it.

'Don't mix them up,' he warned, a thread of laughter in his voice.

'Serve you right if I did,' Polly replied, and resisted the urge to plunge the needle into his leg unnecessarily hard. After injecting the local anaesthetic into the area around the wound and disposing of the syringe, she picked up the other and asked, 'Where do you want the tetanus booster—gluteus maximus?'

He rolled over sharply, eyes laughing. 'No way! I want to be able to sit down. Here will do. I'm going to be limping anyway.' He pointed to his thigh and watched as Polly slapped his leg, swabbed it and injected it with practised ease.

'Not bad,' he said mildly, 'but was it necessary to slap me first?'

'Technically, no, spiritually, yes,' Polly replied, dropping the syringe into the sharps bin. 'Right, let's get you sewn up, *Dr* Gregory.'

He rolled on to his stomach, propped his chin on his folded hands and mumbled something.

'What?'

'I said I'm sorry. I should have told you who I was, but I was enjoying your ministrations and I was afraid you'd flounder if you knew who I was. I didn't mean to tease you at first, and in the surgery. . .'

'. . .it was just too good an opportunity to miss. I know. Right, hold still. Is it numb?'

At his nod, she removed the butterfly plaster, swabbed the wound and carefully trimmed away the softly curling hairs around the area. Then she inserted the suture needle, drawing the ragged edges of the wound together. 'I'm going to do two, I think. It'll be neater. Not that it'll show with all this fuzz.'

'I'll be devastated if I'm scarred, Polly. I'll hold you personally responsible,' he threatened.

'You are in a very vulnerable position,' she warned him. 'If I were you, I'd be very quiet!'

Just then Mike Haynes popped his head round the

door. 'Ah, there you are. Very neat, Polly. Well done. Don't forget to fill in the paperwork so we can claim!'

Polly smiled. 'Oh, no. This one's on me,' she said with a light laugh.

'Can you give me a minute when you're done, Matt?' Dr Haynes asked, and Matt nodded.

'We won't be long.' Polly tied off the suture, clipped it neatly and covered the wound. 'Let me see that tomorrow, and I'll change the dressing,' she told him, disposing of the refuse and stripping off her gloves.

He slid off the couch and dressed quickly, then on the way past, he dropped a quick and meaningless little kiss on her lips.

'Thanks, Polly.'

His smile held his apology, and Polly smiled back her forgiveness. In truth, she couldn't have done anything else, because something inside her had come alive at his kiss, and she couldn't have stopped the smile if her life depended on it.

CHAPTER TWO

THEY met up again at three for the ante-natal clinic, and Polly had an opportunity to see Matt Gregory in action. She found it a real eye-opener.

Far too young to assume a paternalistic attitude, with his warm, open smile and solid bulk he just became everyone's favourite brother. He asked searching personal questions with gentle understanding, said nothing trite or patronising, and managed to refrain from avuncular pats or the worse alternative, chilling professional distance.

He treated the women in his care with respect, interest and a touching tenderness, as if what they were doing was somehow special—which of course it was.

Polly was impressed. She didn't think she had ever seen anyone so *human* before.

Ms Harding, the liberated elderly primip, was dealt with without any *faux pas* on Polly's behalf and with humorous efficiency by Matt, and she was pleased to meet Sarah Goddard, the woman who was going for a home delivery.

When she showed Mrs Goddard in to Matt after weighing her and checking her BP and urine, he asked Polly to stay. As she watched his strong, sensitive hands moving deftly and with infinite care over Mrs Goddard's swollen abdomen, Polly felt some strange emotion rise up and clog her throat.

The baby, resenting Matt's interference, squirmed and kicked, and Matt and Mrs Goddard both laughed, a warm, intimate laugh that made Polly feel left out. The thing, whatever it was, that had come to life inside Polly when Matt had kissed her turned into full-blown jealousy for a brief instant—so brief that Polly didn't even have time to recognise it, but she was aware of a tiny flash of pain which she attributed to a frustrated maternal urge.

Sighing, she turned away and busied herself laying up the instrument trolley with swabs, gloves, KY jelly, speculum, cervical spatulas and the like.

Polly wanted children. She had no particular image of herself, either as a nurse or as a woman, but she knew that men—not all, certainly, but enough—found her reasonably attractive. With her nut-brown hair curling in unruly tangles around her head, and her warm brown eyes in what she saw as an honest but unremarkable face, Polly was as far removed as she could be from her ideal of the Nordic blonde which she imagined was what turned men on. Her breasts were too full, her hips too rounded, although her waist was neat and her stomach flat and firm. She was too short, too squat, and altogether too homespun for perfection, but she knew she had a warm heart and a loving nature, and her one affair had been filled with affection and humour.

Martin had emigrated to Australia, and the choice for Polly had been simple—go with him, as his mistress, or stay. He had never asked her to be his wife, and Polly felt he probably never would unless he was pushed—but she didn't want to push him.

Somewhere inside the practical, cheerful and warm-hearted woman everybody loved to know was a passionate, romantic girl who wanted to be swept off her feet.

No matter that it was unrealistic. Polly knew that in the end she would settle for a kind man and set up a loving home based on mutual affection and respect. She didn't ask for fireworks. She had learned long ago that they were a figment of romantic fiction. All she asked was that some time, before she was too old, she should find a good man to settle down with and raise a brood of chicks. And the young and attractive Mrs Goddard, with her mother-earth good looks and the smooth mound of her burgeoning pregnancy, was a reminder that time was ticking by.

Squashing the thing she now recognised as jealousy, she helped the woman off the couch and back into her dress, before excusing herself and returning to her room where she set about rearranging her shelves.

A few minutes later Matt limped in with two cups of tea, and propped himself on the edge of her desk.

'Are you OK?' he asked, a slight frown creasing his brow.

Polly nodded. 'Of course. Why shouldn't I be?'

'Just wondered. You looked a bit strained while you were fiddling with the trolley, rearranging things over and over again. I just wondered if I'd upset you that much this morning.'

With a sigh, Polly picked up her tea and sank down on to the chair, propping her feet on the desk.

'No. I just felt the pressure of years, that's all. I

was jealous of her—isn't that silly? I think it's all these pregnant bumps around the place this afternoon. You're good with them, aren't you? I get the feeling you really care about those mums and their babies.'

'I do. They're very important to me.'

'You were good with Mrs Major this morning, too. She is pregnant, by the way.'

'I thought she was. She had the look.'

Polly smiled. 'I'm glad you agree that there's a look. Most men dismiss it.'

He gave a curiously bleak smile. 'Oh, no, I believe in the look. My wife had it when she was pregnant.'

Polly felt a strange little lurch of pain. Of course he was married—he had 'HUSBAND MATERIAL' written all over him in letters ten inches high. She should have guessed.

Misinterpreting her sigh, Matt smiled. 'There's plenty of time for you, Polly. How old are you?'

'Twenty-six.'

'Are you? You don't look it.'

Her smile was wry. 'Is that supposed to be a compliment?'

'Just a comment, neither one way or the other. Thinking about it, you must be that old to have enough experience to do this job. But going back to pregnant bumps, you've got years before you need to worry.'

Polly dropped her feet to the floor. 'I wasn't worried, Matt. I just had a surge of maternal feeling—it caught me by surprise, that's all.'

'I know the feeling,' he said quietly. 'Every time I

do an ante-natal clinic, I long to have a child of my own. One day, maybe—but I doubt it.'

'But I thought you said—what happened?'

'She had a water-skiing accident. The baby died.'

'Oh, Matt!' Polly's warm heart ached for him, and she covered his hand with hers. 'I'm sorry. But there'll be other chances——'

'No.'

His bitterness showed briefly in his eyes before he straightened and moved away from Polly.

'Evening surgery,' he said abruptly, and left, limping awkwardly down the corridor towards his room. His tea on her desk was still untouched, and Polly went via the kitchen and took him in a fresh one before his first patient.

He flashed her a distracted smile and busied himself on the computer. He had evidently said much more than he had intended, and now he regretted it. Her dismissal was obvious—and painful.

He found her in the morning, after surgery, when she was clearing up her room and remaking the couch with a clean sheet.

'Morning,' she said, sparing him a quick smile as she bustled round.

'Have you got a minute? There's a patient I'd like to discuss with you, Polly.'

'Sure.' She stopped bustling, and pulled up a chair. 'Go ahead.'

'Her name's Helen Robinson, and I've suggested she comes to see you at the well-person clinic. She's got nothing wrong with her, but she's a real problem.'

Polly's heart sank.

'I've got a letter from her old GP. He describes her as one of his "heartsink" patients.'

Polly suppressed a smile. That had been her immediate reaction, too. She could imagine why. There were patients like that in every walk of medicine—physically apparently fit, but with a morbid fear of their own health or an unrealistic expectation of their bodies. Every last palpitation, twinge or hiccup would send them flying to the surgery in a panic. Perhaps Mrs Robinson was just a good old-fashioned hypochondriac?

'She's in her late forties, not yet in the menopause. She's an attractive woman, slim and apparently healthy. They moved here six months ago, and she's been to see me four times—each time with something unrelated and insignificant. But there's something wrong—some pain inside that shows in her eyes. I don't think she's so much a heartsink as heartsick, and I think she just doesn't know how to start to explain.'

Polly frowned. She trusted Matt's instincts, and if he felt there was something wrong, then there probably was. Not a hypochondriac, then, but was her problem medical or social?

'What makes you think she doesn't need to talk to a social worker or priest, Matt? Why does she need us?'

Matt sighed and ran his hand through his hair, then pulled off his glasses and rubbed his eyes wearily. 'She had a lumpectomy seven years ago for breast cancer, and she was cleared by the oncologist a year ago. I asked her if she had any worries about it returning, and she said no, but she was cagey. Polly, I think something about it is troubling her. She hasn't had a smear done for eight years, and when I asked her she said she didn't think it was necessary. That's when I suggested she should come to see you. I think a well-person clinic is sufficiently routine and unthreatening that you could check all sorts of things without planting any seeds of doubt in her mind. Will you look at her for me?'

'Of course. When's she coming?'

'This evening. I'd like to talk to you after you see her—can you come round to my house? We can have something to eat while we chat.'

Polly's heart hiccuped, and then she remembered the unknown Mrs Gregory. 'Is there any reason why we can't do it here?'

He shook his head. 'No, not really, if coming to my house gives you a problem. The only reason was that I'm off duty this afternoon and I wanted to get my weight off this leg as soon as I could, but it doesn't matter. I can come back quite easily.'

'Oh!' Polly had forgotten his leg. 'Let me do the dressing now and have a look at it—have you got time?'

'I thought you'd never ask,' he teased, but instead of lowering his trousers, he pulled up the left leg to his knee. Polly was relieved. Her feelings about Dr Matthew Gregory were becoming distinctly confused and unprofessional, and that troubled her. If he hadn't been married, well then, fair enough, but as it was—she eased off the dressing, cleaned the wound and redressed it with swift but sympathetic fingers.

'Thanks,' he murmured, sliding off the couch, and Polly, to avoid a repetition of yesterday's kiss, busied herself at the sink.

'I'll come to your house, if you like. What time?'

'When you're ready. I'll be in all evening. Thanks, Pollyanna. I'll see you later.'

She thought about Mrs Heartsink—or was it Heartsick?—for the rest of that busy day, and when she went into the waiting-room to call for her she was able to pick out the woman quite easily, because she had focused her thoughts on her so exclusively.

She was fairly tall, elegantly dressed, with dark hair greying slightly and swept up into a neat bun. She looked like a businesswoman, and Polly wondered if she had been forced to give up her career to move here with her husband, and she wondered why they had moved. Then she remembered that the woman's previous GP and not Matt had described her as a heartsink patient, and she dismissed that idea. Her problem, whatever it was, was longer-standing than that. And Matt was right—it showed in her eyes.

'Come on through, Mrs Robinson,' Polly said with a smile, and seating the woman, she picked up a blank well person card to fill in the details. First, after the name, was marital status.

'I just have to ask a few routine questions, Mrs Robinson. Have you ever been to a well-person clinic before?'

At the woman's headshake, Polly said, 'Well, it's all quite simple and routine. We establish your history, and test all the usual things like blood pressure, cholesterol and so on. Right. What's your marital status?'

'Married,' she answered shortly. Polly thought she detected a twinge of bitterness.

'Occupation?'

'I used to be manager in a travel agency until we moved.'

'Oh!' Polly said. 'How lovely! Did you go anywhere exciting?'

'Once or twice. Nowhere that special. My husband runs his own business, and getting time off is difficult.'

'Oh, yes,' Polly agreed. 'I know several people like that, and they work harder for themselves than they ever would for anyone else. Perhaps we ought to have a look at him too, just to make sure that he isn't overdoing things and doesn't have any problems with blood pressure. This isn't just a clinic for women, you know.'

'He won't come,' Mrs Robinson told her. 'He says doctors are a waste of time.'

'But that's rubbish,' Polly said briskly. 'Without doctors you probably wouldn't be alive now, so he can't say that.'

'He can,' Mrs Robinson assured her, and sighed heavily. 'Sometimes I wonder why they bothered with me.'

Polly frowned. Mrs Robinson was her last patient, and she felt they needed a cup of tea, to break the ice, but she didn't want to do anything which might seem unusual and put Mrs Robinson on her guard. She pressed on.

'Any current medical problems? I gather you saw Dr Gregory yesterday.'

She shook her head. 'I thought I had a chest infection, but he said I was clear. Must have been a bit of a wheeze.'

'Any drugs or allergic reactions?'

'No.'

'What about your parents? Any history of heart disease, diabetes, stroke, that sort of thing?'

Again she shook her head.

'What about you? Do you smoke or drink?'

'Drink, occasionally; I haven't smoked since— well, since my op. I always watch my weight. Glamour is very important in the travel business, and I kept a close eye on myself when I was working.'

'Do you miss your job?'

Mrs Robinson shook her head again. 'No, not really. I miss my friends. It's a bit lonely.'

Polly agreed. 'I've only been here a week and a bit, and it takes a little getting used to. There must be something you could join—perhaps you'd tell me if you find anything!'

They laughed together, for the first time, and Polly felt the ice creak, if not break. She went over the immunisations, recommended a series of tetanus injections, and then reached the tricky bit.

'Do you do regular breast examinations, Mrs Robinson?' Polly asked, and waited while the silence stretched out.

'Sometimes.' The reply was strained, quiet. Polly watched her unobtrusively.

'You're cleared now, aren't you?'

'So they said.'

'What about contraception? You aren't on the Pill, are you?'

'No.' The reply this time came quickly and was abrupt. Polly glanced through the notes.

'Have you still got an IUCD?'

'A coil? Yes.'

Polly made a note on the card. It was like getting blood out of a stone, she thought.

'Periods still regular? No change in flow, or longer gaps, anything like that?'

She seemed to relax a little, as if they had got off a difficult subject. Not for long, Polly thought grimly.

'No changes,' Mrs Robinson said. 'I just tick on, as regularly as clockwork. It's quite reassuring.'

Polly thought she must mean that she was relieved not to be pregnant, and at forty-eight that was understandable.

'When did you have your last cervical smear, Mrs Robinson?'

Immediately she stiffened up again. 'Eight years ago, but I don't need one.'

Polly frowned. 'Eight years is a long time, you know. It's a very simple procedure, and it doesn't hurt at all. I can do it for you, so there's no need for Dr Gregory to be involved unless you would rather he did it?'

'I don't want it done.'

She was emphatic. Polly pressed on. 'Really, you know, it's quite routine. All women from puberty to late old age are at risk to a certain extent, but certainly anyone who is sexually active should have it done—and by sexually active, I don't mean carrying on like rabbits! Anyone with a partner is included, however much their sex lives may have slowed down, or even stopped.'

She didn't reply, but something in her stance alerted Polly. She reached out and took the woman's hand.

'Do you want to talk about it?'

'He hasn't touched me, you know,' she blurted. 'Not since I had the operation.'

Ah! Polly thought. Here we go. 'Why? Is he afraid to hurt you?'

Her high, thin laugh cut Polly to the quick. 'He doesn't care about that. He just doesn't want to touch me any more—he calls me—an udderless cow.'

'Oh, dear God,' Polly whispered, her soft heart torn apart by the pain and anguish in those simple words. Reaching out, she wrapped her arms around the woman and rocked her against her shoulder as the tears fell, released at last after all this time.

'He hates me,' she sobbed, 'he said it would have been better if I'd died. What use am I? All those models lolling about on the brochures, bursting out of their bikini tops, and him going on about going to topless beaches and getting a bit on the side—he hates me, and I wish I were dead!'

Polly had never felt so hopelessly, overwhelmingly useless in her life. She knew that Mrs Robinson had to grieve for her loss, but the way ahead wasn't clear to her, and there were many things she wanted to check up on—like the existence of a local mastectomy support group, or the possibility of reconstructive surgery. In the meantime, she wondered if Mrs Robinson didn't need more than emotional support.

Once the worst of her tears were shed, Polly handed the woman some tissues and slipped out of the door to phone Matt at home and ask his advice. To her surprise and relief, he was coming out of his room, and she grabbed him by the sleeve and hustled him back through his door, pulling it shut behind her and leaning on it gratefully.

She became aware that her knees were trembling and Matt took one look at her and led her to a chair.

'What's up?' he asked gently, and she told him all that Mrs Robinson had revealed.

His face went taut with anger, and he stood up and paced around the room, waves of rage pouring off him almost visibly.

'How could he do that to her? How could anyone say that to another human being? God, Polly, I wouldn't treat my *dog* like that!'

'Do you think she needs anti-depressants?'

He stopped pacing and turned to face her. 'Could be. I'll prescribe some for her if I think she does, just to take the edge off, and only for a few days, and then I think we need to talk about reconstructive surgery—I can think of some surgery I'd like to do to him!'

Polly smiled, and then her smile faded as she remembered Mrs Robinson. 'Do you think he needs help too? Perhaps no one has given his feelings any consideration, or given him an opportunity to grieve. If they didn't have any professional counselling during the time of her illness, then it's not surprising that they can't cope with it.'

'I would have thought all that had been done at the time,' Matt said, surprised, and shook his head. 'We are much more aware now than we used to be about the emotional effects of radical surgery, I think. Polly, see if you can get them to go along for counselling. I've got the address somewhere of the Breast Care and Mastectomy Association—it's a charity, but the work they do is excellent. The head office is in London, but I think there's a branch in Cambridge. They're very good with this sort of thing, and if the Robinsons's marriage is salvageable, they'll probably find a way.'

She nodded. 'Are you going to come and have a chat to her?'

'Yes. Would you mind making some coffee, and then come and join us? I think I'll make more progress if you're there, somehow.'

By the time Polly had made the coffee and gone back to her room, Matt was in there with Mrs Robinson, holding her hand and smoothing the skin on the back with an age-old gesture of sympathy.

'But how would you feel if it were your wife?' Mrs Robinson asked, pulling her hand away.

Matt straightened up. 'I can't tell you, Mrs Robinson, and that isn't really the issue here. How *your* husband feels is what's affecting you, and I think, and Polly agrees, that he's probably very distressed and unable to cope with his feelings. I think counselling could help you, if you want help. You don't both have to go, but of course it would help if you did.'

She lifted her head. 'What about reconstructive surgery?'

'Mammoplasty? It's usually done sooner. What they would do in your case, I suspect, is make a small incision in the skin and insert a silicone implant to help to balance the other breast, and they can create a nipple if necessary using pigmented tissue from elsewhere. Results are variable; usually physically very successful, but it isn't going to cure your marriage problems or make you the way you were before. It's become quite common to do it at the time of the first operation, to reduce the kind of emotional stress that you've been through. In fact, I'm surprised you weren't offered it at the time. Results after this length of time, though, may not be so successful.'

'What do you think are the chances of it working?'

'Depends on the level of residual scarring, shrinkage of the skin and so on due to radiotherapy, and how much was removed. Also the size of the other breast—it's much harder to get a satisfactory result with women who are more well-endowed. I can't really tell you much more without examining you.'

She seemed to shrink into herself, but Polly wasn't about to allow it. Squatting down beside her, she took her other hand and squeezed it. 'I'll be here with you. If Dr Gregory thinks you would be a suitable candidate for surgery, then if you decide that's what you want, he can refer you and get the process under way. Don't give up now.'

There was a long, painful silence, and then she took a deep breath and nodded.

Matt let out his breath in a silent sigh of relief, and stood up.

'Polly, perhaps you could help Mrs Robinson

undress?' he said, moving over to the sink to wash his hands under the hot tap.

Polly watched him out of the corner of her eye, and saw him pick up gloves, look at them and then replace them on the shelf.

'OK, let's have a look,' he said, returning to the couch with a smile. Mrs Robinson turned her head to the side, but Matt ignored her indrawn breath as he folded down the blanket and laid his hands gently on her chest above the breast, working slowly and steadily across it with a gentle, even pressure. When he had finished, he pulled the blanket up over her and tucked it round her shoulders, to restore her dignity.

'The skin seems fairly elastic, and because of the amount of tissue that's been removed it's obviously much smaller than the other one, but luckily your nipple wasn't removed. I think you might get away with it, especially if the surgeon reduced the size of the other breast as well. It could be worth a try, if you want. OK, Polly, would you help Mrs Robinson dress?'

He turned away and busied himself with the notes, as much to give her privacy as anything, and Polly smiled reassuringly at the woman.

'What would you do, Polly?' she asked.

Polly shot Matt a quick look, and gave a small shrug. 'I don't know. Get counselling first, I think. You really don't look that bad to me. There are plenty of women who are naturally that lop-sided without surgical intervention.'

'But I'm mutilated——'

'No!' Polly and Matt both spoke at once, and Matt

continued, 'You are far from mutilated. There's nothing off-putting about your appearance. Believe me, I've seen far, far worse. I don't think you need reconstructive surgery, and if you were my wife I'd move heaven and earth to prevent you going through any more suffering. What you need is help to come to terms with who you are now, both inside and out. Surgery will change the outside, but the inside is far more badly hurt, Helen. You need to learn to love yourself again. Of course I'll refer you if that's what you want, but please try the counselling.'

She nodded, tears welling in her eyes. Polly laid a hand on her shoulder and squeezed gently.

Matt continued, 'I'd like to see your husband, as well, if you can talk him into coming to see me.'

'He won't come. He doesn't care.'

Matt smiled at her, tenderly and with great sympathy. 'Are you sure? Please ask him. If he really didn't care about you, why is he still with you after seven years?'

Matt patted her hand and stood up. 'Polly, have you done a smear?'

She shook her head. 'Perhaps Mrs Robinson would like to come back later in the week and we'll finish off the tests and things? I think you've probably had enough for now, haven't you?'

She nodded. 'I think I'd like to go home and have a bath and an early night. My husband's away until tomorrow, so there's no need for me to stay up. I've got a lot to think about.'

She took Polly's hand. 'Thank you for being so kind to me.'

'Oh, Mrs Robinson,' Polly said with a slight smile,

'you're welcome. I'm always here—come and have a chat if you need to. Don't bottle things up—if you need an answer, come and ask one of us. That's what we're for.'

Polly showed her to the door, and turned to find Matt watching her from the doorway of her surgery.

'Well done,' he said quietly, and Polly burst into tears.

'Oh, Matt,' she whispered, 'why are we so horrible to each other?'

He handed her a tissue and stood patiently beside her while she blew her nose and pulled herself together, then he waited while she found her bag and put on her coat, and locked the surgery behind them.

'Supper,' he said, and with a wink, he hobbled over to his car and climbed in. 'Can you remember the way?'

Polly nodded. 'I'll see you back there.'

As she followed his Volvo estate out of the car park, she thought it was typical that he would have a car like that—big, solid, reliable, safe—just like him. Husband material, she thought again, with a heavy sigh. She wondered what his wife was like.

'She'd better damn well deserve him,' Polly thought with a protective urge, and then laughed, a little weakly. She realised that her laugh was just a short step from tears.

CHAPTER THREE

MATT's cottage was set back from the lane by a wide garden, filled with shrubs and trees and colourful pansies overflowing on to the edge of the path. Polly pulled on to the drive behind him, and switched off the engine, sitting for a moment to gain her composure before getting out of the car. She wasn't sure she wanted to meet his wife, but she didn't have a choice—or did she?

Climbing out of her little Fiesta, she eyed the cottage. It was in total darkness, and Matt was rummaging through a bunch of keys to open the front door.

Was he alone tonight? Perhaps his wife was away—oh, lord, Polly thought, he hasn't brought me back here for some kind of extra-curricular wrestling match, has he? She immediately squashed the idea, and chided herself for her unworthy thoughts.

He needed to rest his leg, that was all. They also had to discuss Mrs Robinson, although admittedly not necessarily tonight, but Polly was lonely, and the prospect of returning to her cold and empty cottage after the harrowing session with Mrs Robinson filled her with horror.

Matt had the door open now, and she ran quickly up the drive and in through the door, smiling up at

him as she crossed the threshold. Then her eye was
caught by the interior of the cottage, and she gasped.

'Oh, Matt, it's lovely!'

Soft pink brick, mellow pine furniture, heavy oak
beams the colour of honey, and plants—plants
everywhere, flowing down off the window-sills and
up the walls, living and vibrant. And it was warm—
a deep core of warmth that reached down into the
lonely places in Polly and comforted her
unexpectedly.

He smiled at her obvious pleasure. 'I like it. It's
been jolly hard work, and I spend all my time on it,
but I'm getting there. I've only really finished this
room and the kitchen. The bathroom's not finished,
and the two bedrooms are still pretty grim, but at
least the bathroom's upstairs now. Here, let me take
your coat.'

She gave herself up to the luxury of allowing him
to stand behind her and ease the coat off her
shoulders, and then watched in fascination as he
shrugged off his jacket, throwing both coats over the
banisters before turning back and placing his warm,
firm hand in the small of her back. The heat seemed
to spread out from his palm and warm her all over.
Curiously, it made her want to shiver. 'Come into
the kitchen. I've put the supper in the Aga.'

As they went through the low doorway towards
the source of the warmth, a black Labrador with a
snow-white muzzle lifted its head from its paws and
sniffed.

'Hello, old girl,' Matt said softly, and crouching
beside her, he scratched the dog gently behind her
ears with one hand while he loosened his tie and

undid the top button with the other. 'Did you miss me, Bella?'

The dog's tail thumped weakly on the ground, and she seemed to smile.

Matt stood up and moved to the sink. 'Poor old girl, she's ancient, and she's beginning to wear out. I know I ought to take her to the vet and have her put down, but somehow I can't bring myself to do it. In her own way I think she's happy. When I feel she isn't. . .' He shrugged, and dried his hands before turning back to Polly.

'It's a hard decision to make,' she said understandingly.

He nodded. 'Come on, there's a chicken casserole in here that's going to be past its best before long.'

He opened the Aga and pulled out a heavy cast iron pot, and when he lifted the lid Polly's mouth watered.

'Gosh, it smells delicious!'

He laughed. 'You don't have to sound so surprised! Here, lay the table, could you, Pollyanna? The stuff's in the drawer behind you.'

Pollyanna again. How did he manage to make the hated nickname sound like a caress? She fumbled in the drawer to give her time to subdue her feelings— feelings that were quite unprofessional and inappropriate towards a colleague and a married man. Especially the latter. Polly sighed.

Matt, mistaking the reason for her sigh, dumped the steaming casserole on the table and hooked the chair up behind him. 'Come and sit down and forget about work. Mrs Robinson is nearer to being happy than she was before she came in, and all thanks to you, so you can put your feet up and relax. Have a drink.'

He pushed a glass of red wine towards her.

'I'm driving,' she protested.

'Not till later. One glass with a meal won't hurt you, and it will probably do you good. Anyway, I can't drink on my own, it's rude, so if you've got any human feelings you'll join me!'

Polly laughed.

'That's better,' he said with a smile, and handed her a steaming plateful of the casserole.

'Ready-cook sauce?' Polly asked mischievously.

His mouth twitched. 'Absolutely. I'd be lost without it. This one's called sheep's eyes in wine vinegar. Bread?'

Polly nearly choked.

After the meal, which was in fact a delicious combination of chicken breasts, chick peas, tomatoes, onions and garlic with fresh crusty bread, they made their way through to the sitting-room and Matt sprawled on the floor, his head propped up on the edge of the settee, legs stretched out towards the wood-burning stove. Polly sat on the chair beside him, with her legs curled up under her, nursing a cup of coffee and watching him as he told her about the renovation of his cottage.

She was amazed. It had obviously taken him almost all the year he had been with the practice, and he had achieved a tremendous amount in that time.

'Did you want to do it all yourself? she asked,

curious for more information about this man who was beginning to fascinate her more and more.

'Needs must,' he replied with a wry grin. 'I'm not made of money, and I had to buy into the practice, find an affordable house and get a reliable car all at once. It wasn't easy. It isn't easy. Sometimes I can't afford to eat.'

Polly ignored his mock-sorrowful face, but asked the question that seemed to arise from his remarks.

'Is this your first practice?'

She was surprised when he nodded. She knew he was young, but as young as thirty?

'How old did you think I was, Polly?' he asked, his mouth twitching.

'I didn't, really. You just seem much older—no, not older, but wiser, if you like—when you're with patients. I suppose it's because you've known grief yourself.'

His face changed, became more distant, and she was instantly contrite.

'Sorry. I shouldn't have mentioned it. I just—you were so good with the mums.'

'It hasn't occurred to you that I could just be a good doctor?'

She smiled. 'Arrogance, Matt?' She clicked her tongue at him.

He laughed. 'I hope not. I had a friend at college. I saw him again a few years later, and he was so pompous I couldn't believe it. I told him not to be so damned arrogant, and he said, "I have a right to be arrogant—I save lives." Can you believe it?' Matt chuckled. 'Pompous ass. Nice guy, though, and he's a damn good doctor.'

'He's right, Matt, in a way.'

'Trash. It's attitudes like that that make people like Mrs Robinson bottle up their fears for so long.'

Polly wondered if he was right. 'How do you see yourself, then?'

'Me?' He stretched out further on the rug, and rested his left ankle across his updrawn right knee. 'I suppose I see myself as a mechanic, really. I just aim to keep my patients in running order, without misfiring or breaking down too often. I try and encourage them to put the right fuel in, and drive in the right gear, and not thrash themselves too hard— it's quite simple, really. If we visualised ourselves as machines instead of immortal and invincible beings, we'd be a lot healthier because we'd be less likely to abuse ourselves.'

'So you don't see yourself as a healer?'

He eyed her curiously. 'A healer? That sounds almost mystic. You know, laying on of hands and all that stuff.'

'But you do, you know. Maybe you don't realise it, but you touch your patients all the time. You hold their hands, touch their arms, rest your hands on their tummies while you talk to them, especially the mums. You did it with Mrs Robinson, too. That was a master stroke, not putting the gloves on. Did you realise what you were doing?'

He nodded slowly. 'Yes. I thought about it. I wondered which she would prefer—a sanitised medical inspection, or a human being telling her that she wasn't untouchable.'

'You did the right thing.'

He raised an eyebrow. 'I hope so. She flinched.'

'Because she hasn't been touched for so long. I would flinch, in her shoes.'

Matt rolled on to his side and propped his head up on his hand, studying Polly. 'How would you feel about looking like that?'

Polly dropped her eyes. 'It would depend on the reaction of my partner, I suppose. If he was like her husband, then much as she feels, I imagine. If I was on my own, then outwardly confident, but very wary in any sexual or emotional context. I suppose it's a matter of trust. How would you feel?'

'It's hard to imagine. I suppose the nearest I could get is an orchidectomy, but they nearly always replace the testicle immediately with a silicon implant. Nevertheless, it's an attack on your sexual identity. Our society is so geared to physical perfection that anyone who fails to meet the standard is automatically going to reject themselves. It's very sad.'

'What if it was your wife?'

'It would depend on the degree of mutilation and the sort of woman she was. I hope I'd be more supportive than Mr Robinson, but I can't be sure that I would cope any better.'

Polly frowned. He was being deliberately non-specific. Why?

'But what if it actually happened to your wife? You married her, you must know how she'd react.'

Matt looked at her strangely. 'It's not going to happen, so why dwell on it?'

Polly's eyes widened. 'How can you be so confident?'

Matt laughed shortly. 'Easy, Polly. People who have been dead for four years don't get cancer.'

Polly was stunned. Dead? His wife was dead? Her eyes filled and overflowed.

'Oh, Matt, I'm so sorry.'

He stared at her in amazement. 'Didn't you realise?'

She shook her head, rummaging in her pocket for a tissue and blowing her nose. 'Sorry, you took me by surprise. I just—oh, Matt. How did it happen?'

'Car accident. It was a long time ago, Polly. I really don't want to talk about it.'

'How old were you?' she asked.

He took off his glasses and ran his hand wearily over his face. 'Twenty six—your age.'

'Oh, God. Your wife and your child. Oh, no. That's too sad.'

'Polly, can we change the subject please?'

She looked up at him, and his face was hard, taut with strain. He still loves her, Polly thought bleakly. I expect she was wonderful—beautiful and generous and kind—Polly sniffed again and dug out another tissue.

'Sorry. It's been a foul day.'

'And you're a softie. Come here.'

She slid down on the floor beside him, and he wrapped his arms around her and hugged her close. She snuggled into the warmth of his chest, thinking of his wife, and his loneliness, and him here doing up the cottage with no one to share it with. He needs a lover, she thought, a wife really, but to start with, someone to hold and share things with, and then later someone to give him those children he wants—

and that explains his comment about never having children, Polly thought.

She tipped back her head to look at him, just as his mouth moved down to kiss her brow, and their lips met, drew apart, and met again. It was a gentle kiss, undemanding, tender, and Polly sighed and eased closer to him.

It was a mistake. With a low groan, Matt rolled on to her, his hips rocking against hers as his tongue plundered the softness of her mouth.

'Polly,' he groaned, and she felt his hand on her waist, sliding up over her ribs to encounter not her soft breast, but a pocketful of pens, scissors, tweezers and the like.

'Oh, God, what is all this rubbish?' he muttered, but Polly was rapidly coming back down to earth.

He was her colleague, a man she had known a mere two days, and although she had a practical and sensible attitude to sex she didn't believe in sharing it with someone she didn't know, even if she did love him.

Now where had that thought come from?

Pushing him away, she struggled to her feet, desperate for some distance between them so that she could sort out her thoughts.

'Matt, we have to stop——'

He groaned, and flopped back down on the floor, staring at her with disbelief. His eyes were bright, glittering with desire. Polly muttered something about the bathroom, and ran up the winding staircase, away from him.

'Second on the left, and mind the floorboards,' he yelled after her.

She washed her face in cold water, desperately trying to cool her flushed cheeks. It was hopeless. Eventually she gave it up as a bad job and went back down. Matt was waiting for her in the kitchen with a fresh pot of coffee and a smile.

He handed it to her, his face curiously blank despite the smile. If she hadn't known better, Polly would have thought that nothing had happened, but she could see the flush still lying faintly on his cheekbones, and his lips were soft and full. Something twisted inside her, leaving her breathless with wanting. Suddenly she couldn't bear the silence, the pretence.

'Matt, I'm sorry. I didn't mean to give you a false impression——'

'No, I'm sorry, Polly, I don't normally come on that strong,' he said quietly.

Polly looked at him frankly. 'Nor do I. We'll blame it on Mrs Robinson and the wine.'

She hugged the coffee. He was leaning on the Aga, his lean hips propped against the towel rail on the front. Polly want to go and stand beside him, close—very close. Too close.

She sat down on the other side of the table and stared into her coffee. She was so absorbed in her thoughts that she didn't notice his approach until he was standing right beside her. Then she jumped and slopped the coffee on her fingers.

'Careful,' he murmured, and blotted it up with a tissue. Then he pulled her to her feet, and wrapped her in his arms.

'I want to take you to bed, Polly. I don't know why. I'm usually much more cautious, but something about you just blows away my reserve. I don't suppose you want to take me up on it?'

She shook her head. She did, very much, but she wasn't going to. Not until he loved her. And he would, one day, if she had anything to do with it.

'I'll just have to cuddle my teddy bear then, won't I?' he said mournfully.

Polly laughed. 'Have you got one?'

'No.' He grinned at her. 'Have you?'

'Oh, yes. He's almost worn out.'

A slow smile spread over Matt's face. 'I'm glad to hear it.'

'Why?'

His fingers traced the little worried frown between her eyes. 'Because, Pollyanna, if you've been cuddling your teddy bear, you haven't been cuddling anyone else. I think I like that.'

'Chauvinist,' she murmured.

'Absolutely,' he chuckled, and tipping up her chin, he dropped a gentle kiss on her lips. 'Take yourself home, Pollyanna, while I'm still prepared to let you go.'

He handed her her coat and bag, held the door open for her and walked her to her car.

'A real gentleman,' she teased.

'Oh, yes. Most chauvinists are. You don't know what you're missing, Polly.'

His voice was like warm, rich chocolate, curling round her senses and making them tingle with anticipation.

'I can imagine,' she said, and her voice was a little wistful.

Matt's features tautened. 'Stay, Polly,' he whispered.

'No.' She shut the door, and wound down the window. 'I mustn't.'

He bent and kissed her again, a light peck that both fought not to extend and deepen. 'Go home, then, Pollyanna. I'll see you tomorrow.'

He stood back and waved, and Polly reversed carefully off his drive and headed home, her thoughts in turmoil.

He was widowed. Available. And lonely, poor man, in his lovely, empty cottage with his ancient dog and his Aga for company.

Polly arrived home, filled her hot water bottle and went to bed as quickly as possible, snuggling down under the quilt with her teddy clutched in her arms.

'Well, Bear,' she said quietly, 'I think it may be nearly time to pension you off. What do you think of that?'

She wriggled down into the bed, and the bear gave a tired groan. Polly laughed.

'I knew you'd agree with me.'

With a smile on her face, Polly fell asleep.

Their paths crossed occasionally during the course of the week, but apart from accidental encounters in the corridor they were never alone.

Until Friday evening, that was. Matt came in to Polly's room as she was packing up to go home, and told her that Mr Robinson had been to see him.

'Oh!' Polly was surprised. 'How did he seem?'

'Frightened. He's still under the impression that she's likely to die, although I told him that after this period of time she's no more likely to get cancer than anybody else. He took a bit of convincing, but once I got him to talk he wouldn't stop. It seems that after the operation his wife withdrew from him, and he didn't know how to approach her. He's been worried sick about her, and all the nasty comments were in retaliation, he said. She's been accusing him of having affairs, apparently.'

'And was he?'

Matt raised a quizzical eyebrow. 'How can you tell? He says not, and I'm inclined to believe him. He's afraid of his reaction—he hasn't seen her without clothes since the op, and I don't think he knows how he'll feel if he does see her.'

Polly sighed. 'They need to make friends before they think about making love. They obviously have a lot to put behind them, but if they both still love each other, perhaps they'll make it. Will he go to counselling?'

'I think so. She's very keen, apparently. It sounded as though they were already starting to talk. He's going to take some time off.'

Polly smiled. 'Well, hooray. One more workaholic sees the light. Is he coming to my well-person clinic?'

Matt laughed. 'One thing at a time, Polly, eh? How's Mr Grey's ulcer coming on?'

'Oh, all right. I changed the dressing on Monday and again today, and it seems to be showing signs of new skin creeping in from the sides. It's so slow, but at least it's not suppurating any more.'

'He thought he was going to lose his leg, you know.'

'Mm. Well, he might have, I suppose. Talking of legs, how's yours?'

Matt grinned. 'Going to tell me to take my trousers off, Polly?'

She flushed. 'Pervert. Can't you keep a professional distance?'

'From you?' He chuckled. 'I'd rather not. I like your healing hands on me, Polly. You know,' he said, hitching up his trouser leg and lying on the couch, 'you're a toucher, too. Did you ever consider medicine?'

Polly shook her head. 'No, I always wanted to be a nurse just because you do get to touch people. I think we've forgotten, in our society, how important contact is. We need to hug and pat and stroke and cuddle.'

'Oh, quite. Would you like to stroke me, Polly?' he asked, propping himself up on one elbow and twisting round towards her, grinning engagingly.

She shoved him back down, surpressing a smile. 'I mean it. It's a part of our language we've forgotten how to use, and in nursing, you get an opportunity to comfort with a touch, a hug—also the caring, the real genuine healing comes largely from nurses, not doctors. OK, doctors can and do perform apparent miracles, but only patient and tender and thorough aftercare gets them through. No, I wouldn't have liked to be a doctor. It's too remote. I like being on the business end.'

She taped a clean dressing over his healing cut, and eased his trouser leg back down over the dressing. 'You'll do. Soap-box session finished.'

He sat up and caught her to him, hugging her

against him so that she was pulled into the cradle of his thighs, her hips hard against him. She put her hands on his shoulders and held herself away, but his linked hands around her hips held her gently but firmly against him.

'What's come over you all of a sudden?' she asked, a little breathlessly.

'Your healing hands, Pollyanna. You drive me wild with desire——'

'At six-thirty on a Friday night? Give over, Matt!'

He laughed. 'You're right, I'm shot. I was just taking your advice about contact, and stealing a cuddle. Have dinner with me on Saturday, Polly?'

Her face fell. 'Oh, Matt, I would have loved to, but I'm going home to my parents for the weekend. I haven't seen them since I moved, and they're going away in ten days on a cruise—six months, lucky things. Dad's just retired, and they're treating themselves. I really can't get out of it, and I wouldn't want to. Sorry.'

He released her. 'Some other time, maybe. I've got a feeling I'm on duty anyway, thinking about it.'

He slid off the edge of the couch and headed for the door, his limp almost gone.

'I'll see you on Monday to take those stitches out, Matt.'

'Have a nice weekend, Pollyanna. Don't forget to take your teddy, just in case you decide to cuddle one of your old flames.'

Polly smiled. 'My only old flame is in Australia, Matt. I'm quite safe.'

He came back and dropped a quick but firm kiss

on her lips. 'I'm relieved to hear it. Give your teddy
my love.'

'I'll do that. See you on Monday.'

She finished up in her room, and headed home to
her cottage to change and pick up her case. By seven
she was on her way, and by eight she had arrived in
Frinton-on-Sea, where her parents had retired.

They were delighted to see her and to hear all her
news, and they stayed up until nearly midnight
catching up.

Polly went up to bed, tired but happy. Her first
fortnight was over, and she felt she had settled well
into the routine. She opened her case, and lying on
the top was Bear. Polly picked him up and cuddled
him.

'He sends his love, Bear,' she said softly, and
lifted her hand to trace her lips with fingertips. They
were still tingling from his kiss.

CHAPTER FOUR

MONDAY came quickly, but not too quickly for Polly. Torn between wanting to see her parents before they went away, and her fascination with Matt and their developing friendship, she was restless and edgy.

Her parents managed to persuade her to stay until Monday morning and leave early, and so she was on the road by six-thirty and back in Longridge before eight, missing the traffic. Her cottage was freezing, so she changed quickly and made her way to the surgery, arriving soon after Angela Raines, the practice manager.

Still restless, Polly busied herself in her surgery, and so she didn't see Matt until she heard his consulting room door shut. What should she do? Go and see him, or maintain her cool and stay in her room?

Maintain her cool, she decided, and was soon too busy to do anything else. Mr Grey was one of her first patients. His granddaughter had stumbled against his leg and damaged the newly healing skin. He was as cheerful as ever, although he must have been in pain, and Polly cleaned the ulcer and re-dressed it very carefully.

'I couldn't be cross with her, poor little mite, but I knew it'd done some damage,' he confessed.

Polly smiled. 'You'll be all right. It's just set you

back a week or so. Not to worry, we'll keep on with
the treatment. Actually, I'm very pleased at your
progress. Just remember to keep moving!'

He hobbled out, and Polly stuck her head round
the door and called her next patient.

It was a baby for the second shot of triple vaccine,
and after taking one look at the infant Polly checked
his temperature.

'He's a bit warm. Has he had a cold, runny nose,
anything like that?'

The mother shook her head. 'Been a bit grizzly
the last day or so, but nothing unusual. I thought it
was teeth.'

Polly chewed her lip. 'Teething won't give him a
temperature. I think I'd like a doctor to have a look
at him before I do the inoculation. He may have an
ear infection or chest infection. Who's your GP?'

When the woman said Dr Gregory, Polly's heart
jumped for joy. A genuine reason to see him! She
slipped along the corridor and knocked on his door.
His 'Come in!' was a little abrupt, and with a slight
frown, Polly opened the door and popped her head
round.

He looked awful. His eyes were red-rimmed, as if
he hadn't slept a wink, and he looked at her as if she
was a stranger.

Crushing the urge to run and wrap her arms
around him and ask him what was wrong, she
dragged her mind back to business and told him
about the baby.

'OK. I'll come and have a look in a minute.'

He turned back to his patient, and Polly closed
the door and went back to her room, puzzled. He

joined them a short while later, and was more distant than she had ever seen him. He was gentle and thorough with the baby, but his usual smiles and camaraderie were definitely absent.

'Your baby has an ear infection, Mrs Howard. I think we'd better give him a course of antibiotics and then look at him again before he has any inoculations.' He scribbled the prescription for Augmentin paediatric syrup, handed it to Mrs Howard and left, advising her to come back in a week.

Polly was surprised. Perhaps she didn't know him that well at all? Maybe his red-rimmed eyes indicated a heavy, boozy weekend? He had been on call, so that was unlikely. Too many calls, and not enough sleep? Many people were grotty when they were tired, she thought, although to be fair he wasn't so much grotty as distant.

The rest of the surgery kept her mind off Matt, and it wasn't until he stuck his head round the door at eleven and reminded her about the ante-natal clinic in the afternoon that she got another look at him.

'Are you all right, Matt?' she asked, her concern showing in her voice, and for a second his mask cracked. Then, almost instantly, his face became impassive and he straightened his shoulders.

'I'm fine. I'll see you at three. I've got some calls to make, and then there's something I have to do at home——' His voice rasped a little, and he turned away. 'Could you get the ante-natal notes out and check them for anything you think you need to follow up? I'll see you later.'

Polly gazed after him in amazement. Where was

the jokey, fun-loving young man of last week? She went into Reception and poured herself a cup of coffee.

Sue Fellowes, the daytime receptionist, was in there propping up the desk and recounting a hilarious tale about a local GP. Polly smiled faintly and stood quietly in the corner, worrying about Matt.

'Something wrong, Polly?' Mike Haynes asked her eventually, and she felt everyone's eyes swivel towards her.

'Matt seemed a bit off today. I just wondered if he was all right.'

'His dog died in her sleep. He found her this morning, and it knocked him for six. Can't imagine why, because he was umming and ahhing about having her put down anyway. Good job, if you ask me. She was his wife's dog—high time he severed the last link. Perhaps now he'll get on with his life.'

Mike turned away and picked up a handful of notes. 'Duty calls,' he said airily, and went out, whistling cheerfully.

Stephen Webster finished signing the stack of repeat scrips in front of him, shrugged into his sheepskin jacket and left as well. Polly, off duty now until her clinic at two, didn't know how to spend the time. Deciding that some food in the house wouldn't be a bad idea, she pulled on her coat and drove down the street to the supermarket.

All the way round she worried about Matt. His wife's dog, Mike had said. Sever the last link and get on with his life. It seemed awfully callous to Polly. No wonder he was so devastated.

She reached the checkout and stared in disbelief

at her purchases. Tins of sardines, a steak and kidney pudding, fish cakes—fish cakes? And tinned peas? Sighing with disgust, she paid for the things she knew she was unlikely to eat, remembered she had forgotten to pick up bread, cheese, fruit and countless other staples, and headed for the door.

After dumping the shopping in her cottage, she drove slowly back into the little town. As she passed the end of Matt's lane, a sudden impulse had her turning in and pulling up outside his cottage. His car was on the drive, and quelling the suspicion that she was interfering, she climbed out of her car and walked determinedly up the drive.

There was no answer to her knock, but when she tried the door, it swung open. Her heart thudding, Polly went in and called him, but there was no reply. She went into the kitchen and found the dog's bed lying in its usual place, but there was no friendly lift of the head or thump of the tail. Poor Matt, how he would miss her. She crossed to the window and peered into the garden. The fine misting rain which had started as she drove back to town was now coming down steadily, and through the grey drizzle she could see him at the end of the garden, shovelling earth into a hole.

He was burying Bella.

Polly turned back to the kitchen and looked around. The dog's bed. Large as life.

Dropping her coat over the back of a chair, she picked up Bella's bean-bag bed and stuffed it into a bin-liner she found in one of the drawers, then she ran out to her car and put the bed, the water bowl and the food dish, still half full, in the boot. Coming back in, she found the mop and washed the floor, removing the trace of footprints and the few lingering hairs, and leaving the fresh scent of lemon on the air. Then she turned to the Aga and put on a pot of coffee, washed up the few things in the sink and tidied up the worktops.

She was hunting in the cupboards for something to give him for lunch when the back door swung open and Matt came in. Startled, she jumped guiltily and looked up at him.

His face was wet, the hair plastered to his head and rivulets running down his neck. He looked lost, utterly defeated.

'What are you doing here?' he asked harshly.

'I came to see if there was anything I could do to help.'

Polly bit her lip. He was scowling at her, his brows drawn together into a frown, his mouth a tight line. His glasses were spotted with rain and she couldn't see their expression, but she would bet her right arm that he had been crying.

He walked over to the Aga and shed his jacket, hanging it on the front rail, and held his hands out to the warmth.

Polly picked up a towel and dried his face, blotting his wet hair. 'You're drenched,' she said softly. 'Sit down and let me get you something to eat.'

'I don't want anything—except to be alone.'

Polly ignored him. 'Here, drink this,' she said, placing a cup of coffee on the table and pushing him towards it.

He sat down heavily, and she made him a cheese sandwich and slid it under his nose.

'Eat,' she commanded softly, but he pushed it away. She pushed it back.

'Damn it, Polly——!'

He stood up so sharply that the chair crashed over on the tiled floor, the noise shattering in the stillness. In the silence that followed, she could hear the faint hiss of the gas burner in the Aga, and the harsh sound of his breathing as he stood with his back to her, gazing down the garden.

She went and stood behind him, wrapping her arms around his waist and laying her cheek against his shoulder. She could feel the shift of muscle as he stiffened, and his indrawn breath lifted her head.

'It's all right to feel like this, Matt.'

'She was just a dog—people die all the time, patients, and it doesn't move me.'

'Of course it does—you just give vent to your feelings in frustration and anger, not grief. This is too close to home for that, but it's all right to grieve, Matt. She was special to you, a last link with your wife——'

'Is that what you think? That I'm all broken up over that lousy dog because she was my wife's?'

'Aren't you? I mean, isn't that part of it?'

He shook his head in denial. 'No. No, Polly, that isn't part of it. I'm all broken up over that lousy dog because I loved her. Nothing at all to do with my wife. Any feelings I had for Elaine were gone years ago.'

Polly was puzzled. 'I don't understand——'

'No, you don't. There's a lot you don't understand about me, Polly.'

'But I thought——'

'Don't,' he advised her sharply. 'Don't think, Polly. You aren't too good at it. You jump to too many conclusions. For instance, I'll bet you have a happy-ever-after image of marriage, haven't you? Roses round the door, two point four kids and nappies on the line?' He laughed bitterly, and turned back to the window.

'My wife was a bitch, Polly. An out-and-out heartless, self-seeking bitch. She killed my child, and then she killed herself, driving recklessly after a party—going home to her lover.'

'Oh, Matt, I'm so sorry——'

He shrugged off her hand, and turned abruptly to face her. 'I don't want your sympathy, Polly. As I said, my feelings for her are long gone, and as for the dog—she's better off this way. I know that. It's just—oh, hell, Polly, go away, would you?'

Polly's heart was aching. She laid her hand on his arm, and this time he didn't shrug her off.

'Oh, Matt. . .'

She wrapped her arms around him, her cheek against his heart. It was thudding erratically, showing her more clearly than his words how upset he was, but he stood motionless, rejecting her warmth.

She didn't know what else to do, how else to reach him, and slowly she stood away, looking up at him with puzzled, hurt eyes.

'Why won't you let me help you?' she whispered.

'Why don't you go and work for the RSPCA? I'm not a lame duck, Polly, and I don't bloody well want to be rescued. Go and save somebody else, eh, there's a good girl? Just leave me alone.'

Defeated, Polly picked up her coat and stumbled

out to the car, unmindful of the steady rain. Once seated, she started the engine and switched on the windscreen wipers, but she still couldn't see. Angrily she dashed away the tears clogging her vision. They were also in her throat, and with a choked cry she bit her lip and headed back to the practice, fighting down the sobs.

Rejection wasn't pretty. It hadn't happened to Polly very often, and she wasn't used to it. Her warmth and kindness had opened many more doors than they had closed, and she was stunned.

'I only wanted to help you, you fool,' she whispered, and then she had to pull over and blow her nose and dry her eyes because she was causing a hazard with unpredictable driving. It didn't help that the road kept disappearing in a haze of tears. A toot behind her forced her to pull herself together, and she carried on down the narrow main street, sniffing and berating herself for not heeding his warning. You can't say he didn't tell you, she reminded herself.

Nevertheless—it was a hard lesson to learn. Polly parked the car, ran into the surgery, thankful for the rain on her face that covered her tears, and went straight to her room, working furiously on the re-arrangement of her shelves to take her mind off Matt and her humiliation. She managed to work up a temper which drove away the self-pity, and then finally hunger penetrated and she went down to the kitchen and found a cup of coffee and a handful of biscuits.

Finishing her snack in double-quick time, she went into Reception, sorted out the notes for her clinic at

two and went back to her room, taking the first
patient with her. By working fast and efficiently, and
somehow managing in the scrum not to lose her gift
of making everybody feel special—a gift she was
quite unaware of—Polly got through the clinic in
good time to assist Matt with his ante-natal clinic at
three.

Clearing away and washing her hands, and laying
out the things she would probably need for the
clinic, she didn't notice the door opening until it
clicked softly shut.

Spinning round, she clutched the instruments to
her chest and stared at him with rounded eyes.

'Are you going to hit me with that speculum, or
just jack my mouth open so I can't abuse you?' he
said softly.

Blushing, Polly turned and put the things down on
the trolley. 'Do you want me for something, or is
this a social call?' she asked, and then could have
bitten her tongue out. Of course it wasn't a social
call.

'I've come to apologise. I didn't mean to be so
cruel to you, but I was feeling thoroughly frayed at
the edges and I just couldn't take any kindness at
the time. I'm sorry.'

Polly turned round slowly and looked up at him.
'Are you all right?' she asked gently, concern fur-
rowing her brow.

He laid his finger on the furrow and smoothed it
away. 'I'll live. Thank you for cleaning up and
getting rid of all the things. I hadn't noticed, but I
was dreading it. You're very thoughtful.'

Polly's heart was singing. Her smile lit her eyes

and warmed her cheeks, softening the expression on Matt's face.

'Oh, Polly,' he murmured, and took her into his arms, hugging her fiercely. 'What have I done to deserve a friend like you?'

His jacket was rough against her face, and she shifted slightly to lay her cheek against his shirt, snuggling closer. With a low groan, he tipped her chin up and claimed her lips, his mouth soft and mobile against hers, warm and tender. 'Oh, Polly,' he murmured again, and then released her with a rueful grin. 'Ante-natal clinic. I must go. Did you get the notes out?'

She nodded. 'They're here. Nothing particularly to follow up, I don't think. I haven't really had time to check——'

'Do it as you go along. I'm sure your eagle eyes wouldn't miss anything important. Are you doing anything tonight?'

She shook her head. 'Trying to get my cottage warm,' she said with a slight laugh.

'Want a hand? You could feed me, if you like. I don't think I want to sit at home tonight.'

Polly's heart, which had leapt with joy, plummeted. She had thought for a moment—but he just wanted distracting. Still, her natural kindness interfered where the woman in her might have rejected him, and she smiled. 'Of course—though goodness knows what we'll eat—unless you fancy sardines and tinned peas?'

He laughed. 'I've got a better idea. I'll pick you up at seven-thirty and we'll go to the pub for a meal, and then back to your place to warm it up together over coffee. OK?'

The smile in his eyes warmed her down to her toes. She had the ridiculous notion that if he smiled like that in her cottage, the wallpaper would curl off the walls and begin to smoulder in response. She chuckled.

'Lovely. Now, what about these mums?'

The clinic was busy. Ms Harding had a slight discharge and so Polly took a smear, and there were two new patients, including Mrs Major who had managed to subdue her morning sickness sufficiently to allow an adequate intake of food. The new patients took longer, because of the history-taking, examinations and so on, and they ran over into evening surgery.

By the time Polly got home there was scarcely time to lay the fire and find something to wear while the water heated up enough for a quick bath. A shower might have made more sense, but in the freezing bathroom Polly decided that she couldn't bear the thought, and so she spent the time while she waited for the hot water riffling through her clothes in despair.

The pub, he had said. Jeans? No, too pedestrian. A dress? But what sort? Slinky, or everyday? Not being spoilt for choice, Polly decided bleakly that everything was entirely unsuitable, and opted in the end for jeans and a lovely designer jumper, a black mohair hand-knit with jewel-coloured leather and silk appliqué and sparkly beads scattered across it.

It was her favourite item of clothing, and her only truly frivolous purchase, but justified, she decided.

The doorbell rang just as she was dragging it over her head, and she stared at herself in the mirror in despair before running to the door. No make-up, hair clustered in damp tangles around her face, wildly unruly as usual, her bare feet curled up against the cold floor, she stood on one leg and opened the door, then gasped in surprise.

Matt stood there, the other side of a huge bunch of flowers, and grinned unrepentantly.

'What's that for?' she asked as he thrust the flowers towards her.

'Just for being you,' he said, the grin fading and a more serious, thoughtful expression taking its place for a moment before the smile broke through again. 'Are you going to invite me in, or are you coming like that, with your wet hair and your bare feet?'

With a confused laugh, Polly backed away and he followed her in, closing the door.

'God, it's cold in here! Haven't you got any heat?'

She shook her head. 'Only the fire in the sitting-room, and it goes out if you don't feed it regularly. Otherwise just a fan heater in my bedroom.'

Matt frowned. 'I've got a Baxi at home, one of those things with the doors on the front. Would your landlord mind if you put it in?'

'I shouldn't think so. I'll have to ask him. There are one or two things I wanted to ask him about anyway, but I don't suppose he'll mind. I expect I'll have to pay to have it fitted——'

'I'll do that for you, idiot! It shouldn't take me

long—I could do it this weekend, if you like. Ask him.'

'I will. It's very kind of you, Matt——'

'Nonsense! Can't have our practice nurse going down with pneumonia, can we?'

So that's all I am to him, Polly thought, and stifled a sigh. 'I'll go and finish getting ready,' she said, and, putting the flowers in the sink, she ran upstairs, hiding her disappointment.

She dried her hair and subdued it a little, applied a quick lick of make-up and tugged on her boots. She was freezing now; the bathwater hadn't really been hot enough and had probably chilled her more than a quick shower would have done. Still, at least she would be clean when she was admitted to hospital suffering from hypothermia!

Running downstairs again, she grabbed her jacket from by the door and called Matt. Following his muffled voice, she found him lying on his back across the hearth, peering up the chimney with a pen torch.

'Shouldn't be any problem,' he assured her, rising to his feet and dusting off his hands.

'You're filthy!' Polly exclaimed, brushing the dust off his shoulders. 'You should have told me what you were doing and I would have given you something to lie on. There, it's not too bad now.'

She forced herself to stop brushing him down, and handed him his jacket. He shrugged into it, ran his hands through his hair and gave a boyish grin. 'Shall we?' He offered her his arm, and she slipped her hand through it and laughed up at him.

'Let's. If only to get warm again!'

The pub was quiet as it was a Monday night, and

they were able to get seats by the log fire which blazed merrily in the end wall. It was a lovely evening, and Polly was delighted that they found so much in common. It was the first time they had been out together, and although Polly reminded herself incessantly that it was just a distraction for Matt so he didn't have to think about Bella, still it had the specialness of a first date. Polly decided to forget the whys and wherefores, and just enjoy the evening for what it was, jolly good fun.

When they left the pub, the rain was coming down again and they ran to the car. The journey back was quiet with a comfortable silence, and over all too soon.

'Now to get your cottage warmed up,' Matt said as he turned into the drive and pulled up behind Polly's little car.

She found the house keys and he took them from her, running to open the door and holding it for her so she could run straight in.

She pretended to scowl at him in the hall.

'You're still limping! I'd forgotten about your leg—what about your stitches?'

'I think they're ready to come out—fancy doing it now?'

'Could do—shall we get the fire going first? It's all laid.'

While Matt lit the fire, Polly filled the kettle and spooned instant coffee into mugs, then found some home-made biscuits her mother had sent her back with. When she joined Matt in the sitting-room, the fire was blazing merrily and he was crouched over it, holding his hands out to the blaze.

'How do you bear it?' he asked.

Polly laughed. 'I don't! It's grim and awful, but there wasn't a lot of choice. I was going to give myself time to decide if I liked working in general practice, and then buy a place in the town if I could afford it. I didn't really intend to live out in the sticks so I would have to use a car all the time, but you have to take what's available.' She shrugged. 'Anyway, in the summer it will be lovely, I expect, and the view is fantastic, no matter what time of year. At the moment I light the fire in here in the evenings, and the rest of the time I carry the fan heater round with me!'

Matt shook his head in disbelief. 'I hate being cold. I would perish here after a short time.'

'No you wouldn't,' she retorted, 'you'd toughen up, like me. The trouble is you're spoilt, with your Aga and woodburner chugging away all the time.'

He laughed. 'I suppose so.' He eyed her sceptically. 'So you're used to it, are you? Is that why you're shivering?'

'Am I?' She knelt beside him on the hearthrug, and handed him a steaming mug of coffee and the biscuits. They ate and drank in silence, staring into the flames, and the fire crackled and spat, the hiss of resin and the sweet smell of apple smoke teasing their senses. Polly leaned against Matt, and his arms came round her, enveloping her in an inner warmth that was nothing to do with the licking flames in the hearth.

He shifted so she was sitting between his legs, his knees drawn up as armrests for her, leaning over her so that his chin rested on her left shoulder.

'Thank you for coming out with me this evening,' he murmured, and his lips laid a gentle trail from her ear to her shoulder, nudging aside the sweater to expose her soft, creamy skin. His breath fanned across her throat, teasing the tiny hairs so that they stood up and shivered. 'Oh, Polly,' he whispered, and eased her round so that she lay against his right shoulder, his left arm coming to rest on her thigh, his hand warm against her hip.

His lips claimed hers, tentatively at first, and then with greater urgency as he felt the quickening of her response. His hand moved up, past the curve of her hip, over the taut plane of her midriff to graze the swell of her breast, and she made a small sound deep in her throat and twisted so that her breast curved into his palm.

It was not enough, and as if he understood, his hand slid away and turned beneath her sweater, dispensing with the front fastening of her bra with a deft twist. Her breasts sprang free, and he stroked first one, then the other with his fingertips.

The slight roughness of his skin drove her wild and she arched against his hand, pleading against his lips. Breaking the kiss, he pulled the sweater over her head and lay her down, kneeling beside her and running his eyes slowly over her body so that she felt the flush run over her skin at his inspection.

Then he lifted his eyes to her face, and she saw the heat of passion in them; holding her eyes, he reached out and dragged his thumb slowly across one nipple, watching her face as it peaked for him. Then he touched the other one, smiling in grim satisfaction as it puckered and strained for his caress.

'My God, how I want you,' he breathed, his voice ragged and taut with control, and then he lowered his head and captured her breast, teasing it with his tongue. Her hands cupped his head, and she threaded her fingers through his hair and pressed him against her, so that instead of teasing he took her nipple into his mouth and suckled it hard.

Tongues of flame licked along her veins, and Polly caught fire beneath his clever, knowing hands. With a cry, she pressed against him, pleading for something—some unknown, unattainable nirvana.

His mouth came up to claim hers, fiercely demanding, and she answered his demands with some of her own, equally intense.

How far they would have gone, heaven knew, but a log fell in the grate, the noise shocking in the silence, and they both jumped.

'It was just the fire,' Matt murmured, but the spell was broken, and Polly turned her head aside as he tried to kiss her again.

'Polly?'

'What are we doing?' she asked in a strangled voice.

Matt laughed, a low, throaty, sexy laugh that melted Polly's insides. 'I don't know what you're doing, but I'm lying here on the floor making love to a beautiful woman, and I don't particularly want to stop, but I guess I'm outvoted. Am I right?'

She nodded, and his mouth came down to kiss her again, gentle, undemanding.

'Pity,' he whispered against her lips, but she felt his smile. 'Is there some frightfully moral reason for this, or am I just rushing you?'

'Oh, Matt.' She struggled to sit up, and dragged on her jumper, ignoring her bra. She eased further away from him, subduing her hair with her hands and pressing her palms against her burning cheeks. 'No frightfully moral reason, but it is rather soon, and I won't be used for comfort.'

'Comfort?' he said, puzzlement in his voice, and then his face clouded. 'Bella,' he said flatly. 'I'd forgotten.'

He stood up and picked up his jacket, pulling Polly to her feet. 'I'd better go.'

'What about your stitches?'

He gave a rueful laugh. 'I think that had better wait until we've both calmed down a bit. One touch of your healing hands on me at the moment, Polly, and I couldn't vouch for my behaviour.' He dropped a quick kiss on her lips. 'Stay here in the warm, I'll let myself out. Thanks for everything today, Polly. You've been wonderful.'

He left her there, and she crossed to the window and watched as he ran to his car and started it, reversing carefully out into the lane. As he drove off, he glanced back and blew her a kiss, then waved. She lifted her fingers to her lips and kissed them, and then blew softly after him.

'Goodnight, Matt,' she whispered.

The cottage had never seemed so warm before—or so empty.

CHAPTER FIVE

HE CAUGHT her in her room before surgery and greeted her with a light, friendly kiss.

'Any chance of having my stitches out?' he asked, and she washed her hands, found the stitch cutters and tweaked them out easily.

'It's healed well,' Polly commented, pleased with her needlework.

'So I won't have to sue you, then?'

She swatted him on the bottom, and Matt laughed and slid off the couch, grabbing her in his arms and catching her against him for a kiss.

'Polly, have you seen—ah, Matt. A word, please?'

They sprang apart, Matt laughing softly, Polly blushing a furious shade of fuchsia and busying herself at the sink as Matt and Dr Haynes made their way out.

'Polly was just taking out my stitches——'

'Novel way to do it—our previous nurse used to use tweezers!'

Their laughter faded down the corridor, and Polly's blush receded with them, but rather more slowly. She avoided everyone for the rest of the day, and was just clearing up after evening surgery when Matt popped his head round the door.

'Can I come in?'

'Only if you promise not to compromise my integrity,' she retorted, and then spoilt it by giving him a warm smile. 'Hi,' she said softly.

'Hi yourself.' His grin was warming. 'Doing anything tonight?'

She laughed. 'Would you believe——'

'Warming up the cottage!' they said in unison, and he tugged her against him.

'Uh-uh! No hanky-panky.'

'Who, me?' he laughed against her hair. 'Would I?'

'Yes, you would.' She pushed him away. 'Did you want something, or have you just come in here to philander with my sensibilities?'

He chuckled. 'I have to go out on a call, to one of the outlying farms. The phone message was a bit garbled, but I gather there's a young woman in labour, having difficulty. Sounds as if I'm going to have to admit her. I'm going out there now—I just wondered if you'd like to come. If it doesn't take too long, we could go back to my place and——'

'If you were going to say carry on where we left off, forget it,' Polly said suppressingly, and then ruined the effect by laughing. 'OK. It might be warmer at this farm than at my place!'

They left together, in Matt's car, and headed out into the country. It was a black and inky night, and there was a heavy frost already at half-past six.

'God knows where this place is,' Matt muttered, peering down a rutted track. 'Is there a light there, among the trees?' he asked.

Polly leant forward and peered through the windscreen. 'Could be. Want to try? There's nothing else for miles.'

They turned on to the track and jolted down the drive—if such it was—for what seemed like an age. Then the track entered a copse, and emerged in a clearing, with a tatty barn on one side and an equally tatty and dilapidated cottage on the other. A pair of lurchers bounded up and jumped up against the doors, baying furiously at them, and Polly shrank back in her seat.

'Friendly, isn't it?' she muttered.

'Stay here, I'll go and find out——'

There was a sharp rap at the window, and they turned to see a tall, thin man in a shabby jacket, a gun broken over his arm and a blackened pipe clenched between his teeth. His mangy beard was stained bright yellow with nicotine. Matt wound the window down, and a great belch of acrid tobacco engulfed them.

'You the doc?'

Matt nodded. 'That's right. I'm looking for Jane Reed.'

'Inside,' he said, jerking his pipe towards the ramshackle cottage. 'Who's that?' He stabbed the pipe towards Polly.

'The nurse. May we come in?'

'S'pose you'd better, since you're here. Wife's idea.' He coughed harshly, and the pipe rattled alarmingly against his teeth.

Lord, Polly thought, it's like a set for a horror film, and she barely suppressed a hysterical laugh. The dogs had got bored and were now fighting in the dirt, rolling over and over and growling ferociously.

'That's enough of that!' the man snarled, and

there was a yelp as his boot connected with a scrawny side.

Matt and Polly exchanged glances. 'You'd better stay here,' he said quietly.

'Not on your life. I'm staying right beside you, my friend. I have the feeling that there's safety in numbers.' Summoning what she hoped was a smile, she climbed out of the car and tugged her coat around her. Matt was immediately by her side, and handed her the maternity pack he had picked up from the dispensary on their way out.

'Right, Mr Reed, if you could show us the way?'

The man grunted and stumped off across the yard to the cottage. When he swung open the door and ushered them in, it was all Polly could do not to turn and run. The stench was unbelievable. The room was piled high with rags, rotting vegetables, opened cans of cat food and the like. Their feet seemed to be engulfed in a squirming sea of skinny cats, miaowing and winding around their legs, making progress across the room difficult in the extreme.

Despite the smoking stove in the chimney breast, the room was bitterly cold and the dirtiest place Polly had ever seen in her life.

'I'll get the wife,' the man muttered, and slammed out of the room.

Matt and Polly exchanged glances.

'I didn't think this sort of place existed any more,' she said in an undertone, and he gave a short, disbelieving laugh.

'Neither did I,' he murmured back. 'I wonder where our patient is?'

'Come on, then,' the man called, and Polly fol-

lowed Matt through the low doorway and up a
rickety flight of stairs. 'Kid's in there,' he jabbed his
pipe, 'I'll be off.'

'Um—Mr Reed, is it? Could you boil some fresh
water in a clean pan for us?'

'Won't cold do?' he grumbled.

Matt frowned. 'Not really.'

'More'n she deserves,' he muttered, and stomped
off down the stairs. Matt opened the bedroom door
and went in.

Even his smile faltered at the sight. On an old
mattress on the floor, amid the piles of filthy clothes
strewn across the room, lay a young woman, patheti-
cally thin except for the huge bulge of her distended
abdomen. She had a black eye, and there was a fine
sheen of sweat across her pale skin despite the
extreme cold. Her hair was lank, her eyes vacant
with pain and misery. She gazed at them blankly.

'Doctor?' An older but equally thin woman
struggled to her feet. She too was pregnant, and
there were other children in the room, sitting about
silently, regarding them with watchful eyes.

'Hello, Mrs Reed,' Matt said gently. 'I'm Dr
Gregory, and this is Nurse Barnes. Did you call us?'

She nodded. 'It's Jane there—I wanted to call you
yesterday, but he wouldn't let me. I had to get you
today, I didn't dare leave it any longer, she's that
poorly.'

While the woman was talking, Matt was crouching
down beside the girl, murmuring soothingly to her.
He tipped a cat off the girl's legs, and eased back
the tattered sheet.

'Polly, open up the pack, could you? I need some

gloves.' He rummaged in his bag for his foetal stethoscope, and held it to the girl's abdomen.

Polly raised an eyebrow, and he nodded his head almost imperceptibly.

While Polly struggled with the pack, Matt took Jane's temperature.

'Hyperpyrexial,' he murmured, then louder to the mother, 'When did Jane go into labour, Mrs Reed?'

'Two days ago, properly, but she's been complaining for days really. I did right to call you, Doctor, didn't I?'

Matt sighed. 'Yes, Mrs Reed, but I should have been here earlier. Your daughter will have to go to hospital, I'm afraid.'

'Hospital? Oh, dear! He won't allow it, Doctor. You'll just have to do the best you can here, I'm afraid.'

And she really was afraid. In the harsh glare of the unshaded bulb, Polly could see the faded remains of bruises on her cheeks and around her hopeless eyes, and she kept glancing nervously towards the door.

The girl groaned and shifted restlessly on the mattress, and Matt turned his attention back to her for the time being.

She was having a contraction, but it was very weak, as if her body knew it was fighting a losing battle. Tugging on the gloves, he spoke softly to her, reassuring her before he examined her as quickly as he could, pulling the sheet back up over her as soon as he was done.

'Malpresentation. The shoulder's wedged across the cervix, but she's very tiny anyway. I would think she's overdue. She'll never deliver vaginally, even if she had the strength, which she clearly hasn't. She'll have to have a section.' He turned back to the mother.

'Mrs Reed, Jane's going to have to go to hospital, or else——'

'Or else what? No damned interfering quack's going to drag my Jane off to no blasted hospital——'

Matt turned his attention to the father, who had entered the room silently behind them. 'Mr Reed, if your daughter doesn't go to hospital, things will be very serious indeed for her.'

He glowered at Matt. 'What d'you mean, serious? Thought you was supposed to be a doctor?'

Matt drew a deep breath. He had no need to dramatise the situation. Rather it was a case of keeping it all low-key enough to get the job done.

'Her baby is already suffering. If she doesn't get help soon, she, too, may be in danger. We have to act now, Mr Reed. You can't struggle with your conscience.'

'He don't have a conscience, the evil bastard——'

'Quiet, woman!' Mr Reed raised his hand and struck his wife hard across the face. She fell against the bed, but struggled up again, wiping blood from the corner of her mouth.

'No, I won't! I've been quiet long enough—too long! I won't stand back and watch you kill Janey! It's bad enough——'

'Quiet, I said!' he roared, and his hand flew out, but Matt caught it, surprising the man.

'Mr Reed, this is neither the time nor the place for a domestic dispute. Your daughter is going to die if we don't get her to hospital fast. Now are you going to co-operate?'

Before any of them knew what was happening, he had snatched up the gun and levelled it at them. 'Just get the baby out—I don't care how you do it— rope it, like a calf, or something.'

Polly gripped the girl's hand and hugged her against her chest.

'Help me,' Jane whispered.

'I will,' Polly promised softly.

'What's that?'

'I said I wouldn't leave her,' Polly lied, staring him down. 'Mr Reed, if we're going to help Jane, we need to get more things from the car. I wonder, while Dr Gregory gets what he needs, could you give me a hand to lift Jane on to the bed?'

'Good idea,' Matt said, picking up Polly's meaning, and while he made his way quickly downstairs, Polly made a great production of arranging the sheets and lifting the exhausted young woman on to the high old bed, while Mr Reed helped grudgingly for as long as Polly could keep him busy.

Matt reappeared, carrying a giving set and a saline drip, and winked reassuringly at Polly.

'Right, let's get a line in and get some fluid into her,' he said gently, and they set to work. Her veins were clearly visible, bright blue against the pallid skin, and the line was soon set up. Matt hung the pack on a nail sticking out of the wall, and checked the rate of flow. 'She needs to empty her bladder, Polly. Is there a catheter in that pack?'

Polly nodded. 'What about him?' she asked, reluctant to submit the girl to any further procedures with her father in the room.

'To hell with him. He won't leave us, anyway,' Matt muttered. 'Just stand in the way. That's it.' With a quick smear of KY jelly, Matt eased in the catheter, and Polly held the bag by the side of the bed as Jane's bladder drained. She frowned at the cloudy urine.

'Is that blood?'

Matt nodded. 'I reckon. Take a sample for testing, can you?' He withdrew the catheter, wiped the area gently and covered her again. 'Does that feel better?'

She nodded slightly. 'Feel sick,' she whispered. Polly produced a kidney dish and Matt held it while Jane retched unproductively into it.

'Poor love,' he murmured, smoothing back her hair.

'Never mind all that mollycoddling, just get the damn brat out!'

Matt was controlling his temper with obvious difficulty. 'All in good time, Mr Reed. We can't do everything at once. Jane's just having a rest.'

'Huh! Up to something, I'll bet! I know you quacks, always sticking your oar in! We're good decent, God-fearing folks——'

'Just shut up, Ely Reed! I've had all I can take!'

In the silence that followed, they all stared at Mrs Reed, huddled against the door post, the great gun up to her shoulder, pointing straight at his chest. There was a click as the safety catch came off.

'You wouldn't know God-fearing if it struck you

down dead! Eighteen years I've suffered you and
your cruelty. Eight children I've born you, and each
one you've beaten and starved—now this!'

'She's evil!' he screamed, 'it's only what she
deserves, the whore!'

'Whore nothing! She was just looking for love!
That's how I ended up with you, and look where it's
got me! I thought you were a good Christian man,
but you're just a fanatic! You make us live like pigs,
trapping us here—well not any more, d'you hear?
I'm through with you! Now back up against that wall
and don't move!'

She held the gun steady at his chest with deadly
intent, and Matt held his breath as the man glared
at her, then backed furiously into the corner.

'He won't give us no more trouble. Do you want
to go and phone for an ambulance, Doctor?'

'I've already done it, Mrs Reed, and I've asked
them to contact the police because I had a feeling he
was going to prove difficult.'

'Difficult? He's always been difficult!'

Polly didn't doubt it. She just hoped that all the
suffering she had evidently endured hadn't unbal-
anced Mrs Reed as well.

Just then she caught a glimpse of headlights
through the trees, and she ran downstairs to direct
the ambulancemen.

'Woman in labour, is it?'

'Yes. Malpresentation. She's been in labour for
nearly three days, apparently. The mother has the
father backed up against a wall with a shotgun at the
moment, so watch your step.'

'Bloody hell!'

And ain't that the truth, Polly thought, beginning to shake. 'I gather he deserves it,' she said wryly, and led them up through the little hovel to the bedroom.

Within a very few minutes the police had also arrived, and after the ambulance had left Matt and Polly went back to the police station with the sergeant and Mrs Reed to give a statement, while the WPC stayed with the children until the welfare department swung into action.

Eventually, at nearly midnight, they were allowed to go, and they drove slowly back to Matt's cottage.

'Nightcap, Polly? I think we've earned it.'

'I think so,' she agreed wryly. She followed him in, the events of the evening etched clear on her mind. 'How do you suppose they'll survive?' she asked.

'Piece of cake without him around, I should think. I expect they'll keep the children in care for some time, but if the father's sent to prison, which he damn well ought to be, they'll probably let some or all of them go home.'

They drank their Scotch neat, refilled the glasses and sat at the kitchen table in silence, each busy with their thoughts.

'I'll ring and find out how Jane is in the morning,' Matt said eventually, and Polly nodded.

'I'd like to know. How do people get like that?' she asked him, her eyes bewildered. Polly didn't want to believe in evil, and tonight had been rather too much of an object lesson.

Matt suddenly realised that she was frightened, all

her previous ideas about mankind challenged by the contaminating influence of one very sick mind.

'Do you want to stay the night?' His voice was gentle, undemanding. 'I've got a spare room and the bed's made up—and it's warm. You'll be safe here.'

She smiled. 'No hanky-panky?'

He grinned ruefully. 'After tonight? I don't think I could.'

Polly shuddered. 'You have a point. Are you sure you don't mind?'

'Of course not.'

'OK. Thanks.' She smiled, and he smiled back, stood up and held out his hand.

'Come on, let's get you settled. You look all in.'

He left her on the landing with the light brush of his lips across hers, and when she woke in the morning it was to the sound of his slightly off-key baritone in the shower next to her room. A few minutes later he stuck his head round the door and smiled.

'You're awake. Cup of tea?'

'Love one.' She stifled a yawn, and he grinned at her.

'Rise and shine, sleepy-head. We need to get you back to your cottage for a clean uniform before the rest of Longridge wakes up and realises you've been here all night.'

'I don't care if they do know,' she retorted with a yawn.

'Well, I do,' he said, and marched up to the bed and tugged off the quilt, heedless of her petticoat.

'Up!' he commanded softly, and she slithered grumbling off the edge of the high bed into his arms.

'Good morning,' he breathed, all toothpaste and soap and fresh, tangy skin, and Polly twisted away from his mouth and hugged him.

'Clean my teeth,' she mumbled, and he chuckled.

'Use my toothbrush—it's the red one.'

And he left her, wondering who else would have a toothbrush in his bathroom.

She went in there, conscious now of her state of undress, and found only one toothbrush. 'Tease,' she said with a little laugh, and looked at his toothbrush for a long moment. It seemed somehow so incredibly *intimate*—with a little shrug, she picked it up.

By the time they had gone back to her cottage and she had pressed another dress and changed, it was after eight and the town was definitely on the move.

'Now everybody will think *you* spent the night with *me*,' Polly said ruefully.

'Wish I had,' Matt murmured.

'Playboy.'

'Chance would be a fine thing——'

'Oh, idiot!' She fell silent. 'Do you really mind?'

He glanced quickly at her. 'What? That people should think we spent the night together? Not for me—it'll probably do my street-cred a power of good! I was thinking of you.'

'Were you?' she said, a trifle wistfully.

He laughed. 'Yes—all night, as a matter of fact.'

They turned into the surgery then, which was just as well as Matt's eyes clashed with Polly's and their message was unmistakeable.

Mike Haynes followed them into the car park, and

his eyebrows rose dramatically as Polly climbed out of Matt's car.

'Sharing transport now?'

Polly blushed, but Matt stepped in neatly. 'We went out together to that maternity case—it was unbelievable. We got back very late by the time we'd finished with the police, so I said I'd give Polly a lift in today, to save her driving home.'

It silenced him on the subject of transport, but Matt's mention of the police caught his attention, and as they joined the others in Reception Matt recounted the full story of the night's events.

'Good grief! Thank heavens you called an ambulance and the police when you did, lad!'

'I wouldn't have been able to if it hadn't been for Polly's quick thinking and calm practicality. She was fantastic.' Matt's smile was warm and generous, and Polly brushed his praise aside with an embarrassed wave of her hand.

'It's just training,' she demurred, but Matt wouldn't let her get away with it.

'Rubbish. You were—are—wonderful.'

'Good job she's not the type to let praise go to her head, or we'd be installing double doors by now,' Stephen joked, and they all laughed, but, although Polly's head wasn't swollen, her heart was bursting with emotion. Not pride, because she wasn't like that, but love. His words went with her all day, warming her and driving away the horror of the previous evening.

Matt dropped in later to tell her that Jane had had a Caesarean section and was now recovering in a side ward in the maternity unit at Audley Memorial, and that Mr Reed had been charged with all manner of offences and was being detained by the police.

'What about the children?' Polly asked.

Matt's eyes were grave. 'Oh, the kids have been placed in care for now. It's a hell of a mess.' His face was sober now. 'How anyone could treat their own children like that——'

He broke off and looked out of the window, his jaw clenched. After a second he relaxed. 'Doing anything tonight?'

'Yes,' she said, 'washing my hair, cleaning my filthy little cottage and ringing my landlord to ask if I can have that fire—can you still fit it for me?'

He nodded. 'Can I bring round a takeaway? It doesn't sound as if you're going to have time to cook.'

Polly sighed. 'Look, Matt, I know you think I'm old-fashioned, but you aren't going to wear me down with persistence——'

'What?'

'Don't look so innocent! I know you just want to get me into bed——'

'Oh, Polly, come on! Give me a little credit. I can take no for an answer.'

'Really?' Her sideways glance was sceptical.

'Oh, forget it. It was meant as a gesture of friendship, a thank you for last night, but if the idea's so repellent to you——'

'Oh, Matt, no! That wasn't what I meant—I'm sorry. Let's start again. A takeaway would be lovely—what time do you suggest?'

* * *

It was a very pleasant evening—spoilt, Polly had to admit, by a distance created by her words earlier in the day. She didn't know how to heal the rift, short of taking off her clothes and making love to him, which would just confuse the issue—and Matt!— even further.

He left early with a brief and very unsatisfactory little kiss goodnight, and she went to bed lonely, unhappy and more than a little cross with herself.

For the next two days he almost ignored her, and then surprised her by popping his head round the door late on Friday and asking her what time he should call round to fit the fire. Her heart leapt, but then she noticed the distance in his eyes, and it sank again.

'Whenever it suits you. I'm in your hands,' she said flatly, and then could have bitten off her tongue when his eyes raked over her.

'You could have fooled me,' he muttered.

'What?'

'How about straight after surgery? That gives me time if I have to go shopping for any bits and pieces.'

'Fine. Thank you.'

'My pleasure.'

And that was the end of that stilted little interview!

Polly went home and slammed and crashed around in a paddy for a while, then the phone rang. Matt! she thought, her heart leaping hopefully, but it was her mother, frantic.

'Darling, you've got to help us! You know the Williamses were going to have Taffy? Well, they've been offered a friend's villa in Marbella for six weeks after Christmas, and they want to go, so they can't have him. I don't know what to do—I'm at my wit's end. I can't bear the thought of putting him into kennels, especially in the winter. It's so cold, and he'll be miserable, but I don't know what else to do. Are you *sure* you couldn't have him?'

'Oh, dear, Mum. Well, I could ask my landlord— I spoke to him earlier in the week, and he was very helpful, so perhaps he won't mind for a short while. I know the lease says no pets, but—leave it with me, Mum, and I'll come back to you.'

Polly rang her landlord, but with no joy. He was adamant—not even a hamster. Disheartened, she rang her mother back. 'No go, Mum. I just can't help—unless—remember I told you Matt Gregory had a dog? Well, she died, and I know he misses her. Perhaps he'd have Taffy till you come back? Look, I'm seeing him tomorrow, I'll ask him and let you know. I'm sure he'll say yes.'

But in the morning Matt was late after surgery, and grumpy when he did arrive, so that Polly didn't like to broach such a sensitive subject.

She fetched and carried, helping him to bring the parts of the fire in while he carried the stove itself single-handed and rejected her offer of assistance. She was in the kitchen making them some lunch while he swore and struggled in the sitting-room, when her parents pulled on to her crowded drive.

A beautiful golden retriever leapt out over her mother's lap, and dashed up to the door to greet her.

'What are you doing here?' Polly squeaked, frantic.

'Well, we're leaving so early on Monday we thought it would be just as well to get this bit over with. Bless you for sorting it out.'

'But Mum, I haven't——'

'Sorting what out?' Matt asked, appearing at her shoulder looking like a chimney sweep.

Polly closed her eyes in defeat. 'Mum, I'd like you to meet Matt Gregory. Matt, this is my mother, Marjorie Barnes, and my father Douglas——'

Matt held out his hand, looked at it ruefully and laughed. 'Pleased to meet you.'

'And you—and this, of course, is Taffy.' She indicated the dog, who was by now washing Matt's hands and squiggling ingratiatingly at his feet. 'Dr Gregory, I can't tell you how grateful we are to you for having him while we're away.'

Matt's eyes rose to Polly's, and his jaw dropped slightly.

'I was going to ask you——'

'I was so sorry to hear about your dog, but it's a blessing in disguise for us,' Mrs Barnes rushed on, oblivious to the undercurrents flowing between Matt and Polly. 'He's taken such a liking to you, as well. I'm so glad we've had a chance to meet you, Dr Gregory——'

'Call me Matt,' he said, and resignation settled on his features. 'I'm pleased to meet you, too. As for you——' he looked down at the dog, whose ears he was absent-mindedly fondling '——it'll be my pleasure.'

'Are you sure?' Polly's mother asked earnestly, and Matt nodded.

'Yes, Mrs Barnes, I'm sure.'

Polly let her breath out on a sigh of relief. She hadn't realised that she had been holding it. Matt's glare had her catching it again.

Her father was dragging all the dog's things out of the car and carrying them inside. 'I'll leave these here, shall I, darling? We have to be on our way—tons to do and the place is in chaos.'

He kissed her cheek, shook hands with Matt and ruffled Taffy's fur. 'Now you be good, you old rogue!' he said gruffly, and Taffy obediently went and sat beside Matt, grinning up at him.

'Look, they're going to be great friends, Doug!' Mrs Barnes said happily, and Polly closed her eyes.

So they might be, Polly thought, but she wondered if she and Matt would ever be friends again!

CHAPTER SIX

HE WAS, predictably, furious. Polly apologised—or tried to, but he cut her off with a chopping movement of his hand, turning away and going back into the sitting-room to wrestle with the fire.

He refused lunch, and carried on fitting the fire with the intervention of Taffy, who thought Matt was lying on the floor for his benefit and kept jumping on his chest and growling playfully.

'Get that damn dog out of here,' he snarled in the end, and Polly removed the exuberant hound to the kitchen and shut him in.

'Matt, let me explain——'

'No,' he said curtly. 'There's nothing to explain. You've landed me with that wretched animal without so much as a by-your-leave, and now you think you can explain?'

He sat up and cracked his head on the fireplace. 'Damn it, Polly, just shut up and leave me alone! If you want to do something useful, I could do with a drink.'

Chastened, she brought him a cup of coffee, handed it to him in silence, and went miserably back into the kitchen, sitting on the floor with Taffy and hugging him for comfort.

A short time later Matt came out and demanded newspapers. Polly silently handed him a stack, and he went back into the sitting-room, emerging seconds later for matches, then for kindling and coal.

She followed him the last time, and watched as he laid the fire, stuck in a match and closed the doors. Almost instantly a cheerful glow erupted behind the glass panels, and Polly sighed with relief.

'You control it here, with this wheel—this way to shut it down, this way to open it,' he demonstrated, and then stood up.

'Thank you, Matt,' she said quietly, not knowing quite how to deal with him in this mood, and riddled with guilt besides.

'You're welcome,' he said, without a trace of sarcasm, which of course made her feel worse.

'Can I help you put the dog's things in the car?' she asked, and caught her bottom lip between her teeth as she waited for the answer.

'I think you've helped enough,' he said eventually, and this time the sarcasm did creep in. Effectively silenced by it, Polly stood helplessly by while he loaded his tools into the car, picked up the dog's bed and assorted dishes, food et cetera and piled them into the back. 'Come on, Taffy,' he said with gentle resignation, and with a little whine and an anxious glance at Polly, Taffy left her side and jumped into the car.

Matt slid behind the wheel without looking at her, and drove off without a backward glance.

'Damn him,' she muttered, trailing miserably back into the sitting-room. The fire was crackling cheerfully, and she huddled over it, horrified by how badly everything had gone wrong. She carried his mug out to the kitchen to wash it, and found that the sooty grime wouldn't rinse off. Trying to shift it, she squirted washing-up liquid on it, and it slid out of her hands and shattered in the bottom of the sink. She picked up the pieces and tried to put them together again.

'All the king's horses and all the king's men,' she whispered. It was like all her hopes for their fragile relationship, smashed beyond repair.

Polly burst into tears.

It was a moment before Polly realised what had woken her, and then another moment before she could bring her sleep-numbed limbs into action.

She stumbled down the stairs, grabbing the banister, and snatched the phone off the hook.

'Hello?'

'Polly?'

'Matt? What's wrong?'

There was an exasperated sigh, and a miserable whine. 'All right, Taffy. Good boy. Polly, this damn dog of your mother's won't stop crying, and I'm at the end of my tether. Do you think you could come and sort him out?'

Polly blinked at her watch. Three-fifteen. Good lord! 'I'm coming,' she mumbled.

Dragging on her jeans and a thick sweater against the biting cold—less biting, she had to admit, with Matt's fire; she must remember to thank him—she grabbed her coat and car keys and ran out into the frosty night.

There was ice on her windscreen, and she cursed the lack of a garage while she scraped at it with a spatula. Of course it would have been less unpleasant with gloves on, but she couldn't find them!

With just enough screen clear for safety, Polly made her way slowly round to Matt's, shivering violently. By the time she arrived the heater was just starting to work. 'Useless heap,' she grumbled affectionately and stumbled up the path.

The door was snatched open as she reached it, and a joyful Taffy threw himself at her, paws on the chest, almost knocking her down. Matt grabbed her to steady her, and practically hauled her into the house. He was wearing a towelling robe which stopped at mid-thigh and was just about held together by the belt. A tangle of dark curls showed in the deep V of the neck, and his bare, well-made feet were planted squarely on the hall floor. His jaw was rough with stubble, accentuating the raw masculinity that poured off him in waves. It was accompanied by exasperation.

'Thank God you're here. He's been howling and whining, and he wouldn't let me near him—stupid mutt.' He rumpled the dog's ears affectionately, and a long pink tongue shot out and slurped his hand.

Matt closed his eyes. 'My reward, I suppose, for fetching you. Right, you know where everything is— I'm going back to bed.'

With that he turned on his heel and padded back up the stairs, his long, well-muscled legs with their heavy dusting of hair rising past her eye level as he went up, drawing her gaze like a magnet. Polly groaned. Now was not a good time for her hormones to kick in!

Turning to the wretched dog, she dragged him into the kitchen.

'Bed!' she commanded, and tail between his legs, he slunk into the bed with his head low, peering up through his eyebrows.

'Don't look at me like that!' she told him crossly. 'You've got me in more trouble than I care to think about, and I'm not having any of that emotional blackmail stuff. You can just stay there and be miserable quietly on your own!'

With that she stalked off, following Matt up the stairs and going into the room she had occupied before. The bed had been neatly remade, and she tugged off her clothes and slid gratefully between the crisp white cotton sheets with a sigh. Bliss, she thought.

It was not to be. Just as she was dropping off, there was a scratching at the door, followed by a heart-rending whimper.

'Taffy, go to bed!' she whispered loudly.

There was a second's silence, and then another whimper, followed by another scratching noise.

'Damn,' she muttered, and sliding out of bed, she opened the door. 'Taffy, go and—Taffy!'

The wretched dog leapt on to the bed, turned round and round, and settled down right in the middle of the couterpane, leaving Polly a choice of sides—both cold!

'Shove over, wretch!' she hissed, and humped his body across the bed a little. Then snuggling back down, she curled herself around his body and fell asleep, lulled by Taffy's snores.

That was how Matt found them in the morning.

With a sigh of resignation, he pulled on his track suit and whistled softly. Taffy's ears came up, followed by his head, and great eyes gazed at Matt soulfully.

'Come on, boy! Good dog,' Matt whispered, but Taffy declined, and tucked his nose under his paws. 'Walkies?' he tried, and with a single bound Taffy was at his side, tail lashing, great jaws grinning. Matt rolled his eyes. 'Come on, then.'

Polly, freed from the pressure of Taffy's body, rolled into the middle of the bed and sighed with relief. Her left arm was outflung, her slim, pale shoulders unbearably tempting above the hem of the sheet. Dragging his eyes away, Matt closed the door softly and took the bounding dog downstairs.

When they got back, Polly was sitting in the kitchen nursing a cup of tea.

Catching a glimpse of them coming down the lane, she opened the front door and stepped out into the glorious sunshine. Everything sparkled in the sun, and there was a fresh, clean, cold smell to the air. Polly drew in a deep breath, then let it out slowly. Matt and Taffy were just turning on to the drive, and her heart lurched as she watched them. Despite his reluctance, Matt seemed to be getting on well with the dog. As for Polly—she really must try again with Matt.

'Morning,' she called gaily. 'There's tea in the pot. What do you want for breakfast?'

'Anything. I'm starving. Lack of sleep does that to me,' Matt said wryly.

'I would have slept all right if it hadn't been for someone who insisted on hogging the middle of the bed!' she said with a laugh, glowering at the dog.

'You looked quite happy to me,' Matt retorted, lips twitching. Polly was so busy trying to work out if he was still cross that she didn't hear the footsteps approaching until they drew level with the gate.

'Morning, Dr Gregory, morning, Nurse! Lovely morning!'

Matt froze, then turned slowly while a flush crept up Polly's cheeks. 'Wonderful, Mr Grey. Nice to see you about. Off to church?'

'That's right.' The elderly man leant on the wall to get his breath. He pointed at Taffy with his stick. 'Got a new dog, Doctor? I was sorry to hear about old Bella.'

'Oh, well, actually Taffy belongs to Nurse Barnes. He's just visiting.'

'I see!' Mr Grey's rheumy old eyes twinkled wickedly, and Polly's blush deepened. 'Well, have a nice weekend, you two. Good to see you young people having some fun—all work and no play, and all that! See you around!' With a wave of his stick he moved on, leaving Polly and Matt open-mouthed on the drive.

With a sigh, Polly sagged against the door.

'I wonder what he heard?' she groaned.

'Everything, judging by the twinkle in his eye,' Matt said with a chuckle.

Polly groaned again. 'How can you joke about it? It'll be all round the town by lunchtime. I can hear it now—that nice young Dr Gregory's got himself well set up with that little nurse—damn, damn, damn!'

Matt laughed. 'What's wrong, Polly? Didn't you want to be seen with me?'

'That's not what I meant, and you know it! I wouldn't mind so much if we *were* having an affair, but all those comments about not having much sleep, and somebody hogging the bed! All that ammunition, and you have to go and shoot yourself in the foot!'

Matt laughed again, and ushered Polly inside. 'No smoke and all that. I'd like us to be having an affair, but someone round here won't play ball.'

'Yes, well, I'm not into ball games,' Polly said crossly, and then blushed at Matt's disbelieving splutter of laughter. 'I didn't mean that—oh, shut up and have some tea. I'm going home.'

'Hang on, Polly—I'm sorry.' Matt took her shoulders between his large, firm hands, and kneaded them gently. 'Kiss and make up?' he murmured.

'Will you forgive me for landing you with the dog? Mum's friends were going to have him, but at the last minute they couldn't, and my grotty landlord said I couldn't have him either, and I thought—well, I thought you missed Bella.' Her eyes sought his, and what she saw there reassured her.

'I do—but for all sorts of reasons, not least of which being that she was there when I needed a willing ear—and dogs are very unjudgemental. However, I was also enjoying my freedom, after all this time. They're a bit of a tie, and I suspect this young scallywag will be more demanding than old Bella was. Not to worry—we'll be fine. He was good company this morning on my run.'

'Run? Oh! I thought you'd been for a walk!'

Matt grinned. 'Well, I did walk the last little bit,

but only because my leg stiffened up. It's still a bit tight where the stitches were, so I'm taking it steady. Now, how about some breakfast? I really am hungry—and later on this morning I want to pop into the Audley and see Jane Reed and her baby. Want to come?'

Polly beamed. 'Love to. Breakfast coming up.'

'But not before my kiss, Pollyanna,' he murmured, and pulled her unresisting body into his arms.

They were ushered into a side-ward in the maternity unit of the Audley Memorial Hospital, where an almost unrecognisable radiant young woman was sitting up in bed, a tiny baby held to her breast. A young man was bending over her, coaxing gently.

'Come on, little one,' he urged, 'suck a bit—there's a good lad!'

Matt coughed quietly, and the absorbed young couple jumped.

'Doctor! And Nurse! How nice to see you. Come on in. Here he is—wretched little scamp. He won't feed.'

Polly smiled. 'I'm sure he will—it's just a question of technique. He's lovely, isn't he, Matt?'

Matt made his way to the head of the bed, perched on the side, and took the baby's feet in his hand. 'He's tiny—gorgeous. He seems to have survived his sticky start. What about you? Everything all right?'

Jane sighed contentedly. 'Yes, fine. Or it would be, except he won't feed, and they're threatening me with the milking machine again. Honestly, I feel like one of Richard's cows!'

'That won't be necessary,' Matt said with a grin. Polly watched, fascinated, as he took over. She knew that Jane's baby had been in special care for the first few days, and that they had used the breast pump to get Jane's own milk for him. The changeover from tube or bottle to breast was often difficult. He gripped the baby's head firmly. 'Brush your nipple against his cheek, and he'll turn towards it with his mouth open—then you push his head hard against you, and hey presto—try it—no, like this—there! Feel it?'

Jane winced, and laughed. 'All the way down to my toes,' she said breathlessly, and looked down in wonder at the tiny mouth sucking greedily from her breast. 'He's doing it, Richard!' She looked up at Matt, her eyes filling with tears. 'I nearly lost him— I can't tell you——'

'Shh.' Matt squeezed her hand. 'He's our reward. That's all we need.'

'I've got lots to tell you. First, I'd like you to meet my boyfriend.'

Matt and Polly both turned to the young man who was standing back now, hesitantly twisting and untwisting a scrap of paper.

'Thanks for what you did for Janey,' he blurted, and stuck his hand out.

Matt shook it. 'You're welcome. I take it you have a vested interest?'

The ghost of a smile played across the young man's face, and he blushed and nodded. 'We're getting married, just as soon as we can. Mr Fairchild, my boss—he's got the farm next to the Reeds'—he's got a little bungalow on the farm; he used to use it as an office, but his kids are grown up now and the big house is almost empty, so he said he'll move his office up there again and let us have the bungalow. It's nothing special, but he's said he'll buy the paint and let me decorate it, and he'll put in some carpet of sorts from the house. He won't charge us much rent, but he said something about a wage increase, and maybe even make me farm manager if I do an accounts course at the college next year.'

The long speech over, he lapsed into embarrassed silence.

'It's a big responsibility,' Matt said quietly.

'I don't mind,' the lad said firmly, 'I love Janey. Nothing's too much to do for her. I would have married her before, but her father wouldn't let us. Well, she's eighteen soon, so he can't stop us then.' His jaw jutted with determination, and Polly glimpsed the steel behind him. He was going to be a fine young man, and Jane would flourish under his love and care.

Matt regarded them both in thoughtful silence.

'He does love me, Dr Gregory,' Jane said with quiet conviction.

'I'm sure he does. And I'm sure he'll cope very well with the responsibility, too.'

His finger grazed the baby's cheek tenderly. 'He's gone to sleep. Does he have a name?'

Jane smiled shyly and flushed a little. 'Not yet. We thought—we were going to ask you yours.'

'Mine?' Matt gave an embarrassed little laugh. 'Matthew—but don't feel obliged to like it!'

'Matthew Hollingwood—goes rather well, doesn't it, Richard?'

He nodded. 'Sounds a fine name. Bit of a mouthful for such a tiny thing. Hello there, little Matthew! What d'you think of that, then, son?' Richard moved to sit beside Jane, his arm round her shoulders, gazing down at their son. They made a lovely family group—a touch too young, perhaps, but with all the vital ingredients.

After saying their goodbyes, Matt and Polly left, both too choked to speak. It could so easily have gone horribly wrong for those young people, and yet somehow everything was falling into place.

'I just hope they know what they're doing.' Matt's words cut in on Polly's thoughts, and she was shocked at the thread of bitterness in his voice.

'Why shouldn't they?'

'Because they're getting married for all the wrong reasons——'

'The baby, you mean? He looked like a pretty good reason to me!' Polly retorted defensively.

'Huh! Worst reason in the world to get married.'

'Just because you——'

'Yes?' Matt stopped in the corridor and turned Polly to face him. 'Just because I what?'

Polly shook her head. 'Nothing.'

'Now listen,' Matt said furiously, turning her face back to his, 'you know nothing at all about my marriage—nothing!'

'So tell me!' Polly shouted.

'No—not here, not now, and certainly not at the top of my voice in a hospital corridor!' he yelled.

'Shh!' someone hissed, and Polly suddenly became aware of all the curious glances.

Tears stinging behind her eyes, she marched off

down the corridor, shrugging of Matt's hand when he tried to catch her up.

'Suit yourself, but you're going the wrong way,' he said, and turned on his heel, leaving her stranded.

Swallowing her pride, she ran after him.

'Wait, Matt,' she said, her voice catching. 'I'm sorry. I didn't mean to criticise you, but I can't help feeling that your bad experience has coloured your judgement——' She faltered under his glower, but struggling to keep up, she carried on, 'I just want them to be happy.'

He stopped again, and sighing, turned to her. 'So do I, Polly. But there's the difference between us. You *expect* them to be happy, whereas I. . .'

'Yes?'

'I expect them to fail,' he said heavily, and walked on, his shoulders slumped in defeat.

You, Dr Gregory, are going to believe in happy endings, Polly said to herself, or I'm going to die in the attempt.

Then gathering up her resources, she straightened her shoulders and followed him out in the clear winter sunshine, her faith like a bright mantle around her heart.

Despite his pessimism, their own relationship seemed to deepen and develop after that. Maybe Polly's faith was working, maybe it was the Christmas spirit, but as November faded into December, and the season of goodwill approached, they developed a comfortable working relationship and a deep personal friendship.

Taffy helped, of course, with his boundless

energy. They took him for long energetic walks through the woods at the other side of Polly's river, and would often go back to her cottage for tea and crumpets over the fire which Matt had installed and which had proved a godsend. Sometimes when Matt and Taffy went out for a run in the mornings they would see Polly in her window and pop in for a cup of tea to start the day.

And lovely days they were, clear and bright—often cold, but sunny and dry, and they were able to get out and about whenever they weren't working.

They were accepted as a couple, not only by the other members of the practice but also by the townsfolk who loved a good romance, especially coming up to Christmas.

Mr Grey, who of course had misunderstood totally their conversation on the drive that fateful Sunday morning, was obviously delighted with the developments. 'How are you and your young man getting on, my dear?' he would ask when he came in to get his ulcer dressed.

'He's not my young man, Mr Grey,' Polly would reply, but his eyes would twinkle and Polly would blush and it was pointless trying to deny it to him.

Even more pointless denying it to herself, because as far as Polly was concerned, Matt had her heart and there was an end to it. She was fairly sure that she had his, too, but he was still very wary, and unwilling to make any kind of commitment.

Although their evenings out—usually two or three a week, depending on the on-call rota—usually ended up with a kiss and a cuddle, it never went further than that, by mutual consent.

Matt seemed to realise that Polly would never give herself to him without a commitment, and as he was unwilling to make one it seemed fairer to both of them to keep the relationship stable.

Fair, but frustrating, for both of them. Matt often ran Polly home and then took Taffy out for a long walk through the winding lanes around the little town centre, walking off his inceasing need for her, while Polly would lie awake and wonder why she was being so self-sacrificing.

The practice Christmas party was to be held at Mike Haynes' house, and everyone bar Matt and Polly would be there with their partner. It was taken for granted by everyone that Matt and Polly would be together. Neither of them had really given it a thought until the week of the party, when Matt had come into Reception during Monday morning in time to hear Sue, the receptionist, dictating a list of names to Mike's wife Anne over the phone.

'Stephen and Jill, Angela and Bob, me and David, naturally; I think Kay will be coming with her neighbour—they're seeing a lot of each other, but I will just check, Anne—oh, and Matt and Polly, of course.' There was a pause, and Sue laughed. 'Oh, I think so. Could very well be! Fine, Anne, I'll see you.'

'Could very well be what?' Matt asked as she put the phone down.

'Oh! Hello, Matt, I didn't see you. What did you say?'

'"Oh, I think so. Could very well be," I think were your exact words. You were talking about me,

Sue—or me and Polly, more precisely. Come on, spit it out!'

Sue had the grace to blush. 'Anne asked if you were serious about each other.'

'Is that a fact?' She blushed again, and Matt relented. Anne was well known for her earthy sense of humour, and he thought it prudent to let sleeping dogs lie. 'We will be coming to the party together, if that was what you wanted to know.'

Stifling a grin, he turned away and busied himself signing repeat prescriptions, and recounted the conversation to Polly later in the day.

'Do you mind them taking our togetherness for granted?' Polly asked him seriously.

In answer, he tugged her into his arms and kissed her soundly. 'Not at all, Pollyanna. Why should I? By the way, while I think about it, Mrs Reed is coming in to see me this afternoon for the ante-natal clinic. I went to see her last week—she's left him, moved into town, into one of the council houses. It seems incredible, with all the talk of housing shortages, but apparently this one has been standing empty, so she was able to go straight in. She's got the children back, and they're settled in school again without any problem, but I'm worried about her. She's taking on a tremendous load. I gather social services have been very supportive, and she's been given furniture, bedding and so on. It's no show house, but it was as neat as a new pin.'

Polly was impressed. 'That's terrific. I wondered how she was getting on. What about him?'

Matt shook his head. 'He's out pending trial, but they've got a court injunction preventing him from

going to the house or harassing her, so she feels
fairly safe. I think they'll probably refer him for
psychiatric treatment in the end. He's not danger-
ous, but he's certainly fanatical.'

'Were the kids abused, do you know?'

'Sexually, you mean?' Polly nodded. 'No, not as
far as I'm aware. Mrs Reed didn't say so, and she
said plenty of other things! I don't think she would
have held back.'

Matt glanced at his watch. 'Going home to let
Taffy out—got time for a quick bite?' He nibbled
her neck suggestively.

'No, Count Dracula, I haven't,' Polly said with a
laugh, and pushed him away.

She made a drink, grabbed a biscuit and hurried
through her surgery so that she had time to get out
the notes for Matt's ante-natal.

The first patient was Mrs Goddard, who was
showing signs of readiness. 'Head's engaged,' Matt
said with satisfaction, and patted the smooth curve
of her abdomen. 'Soon be seeing you, won't we?' he
said to it, and Mrs Goddard laughed.

'Just as long as I make it through my Christmas
shopping,' she said, and he frowned.

'I wouldn't go too far, and I wouldn't go alone,
not now. You're very close, and you know what
you're like!'

She gave a rueful smile. 'I had a feeling you were
going to say something horribly sensible like that!
My husband would skin me if I went out by myself.
Thank God he's able to bring work home, because
the other three are really too much for me now.
They break up from school and playgroup this week,

so I'll have them all day, every day.' She grimaced, and Polly chuckled.

'Surely they can't be that bad?'

Her eyebrows shot up. 'How many have you got?' she asked.

Polly flushed. 'None—and I take your point!'

Sarah Goddard grinned. 'They're OK. They just run everywhere!'

'Yes, well, don't try and keep up at the moment!' Matt cautioned with a smile. 'Go on, go away and look after yourself—better still, get Tim to do it for you!'

The energetic and self-contained Ms Harding was next, fit as a flea and thoroughly enjoying her pregnancy. 'We've enrolled for NCT classes, starting in January. We're both really looking forward to it, and the baby. Funny, I wouldn't have had either of us pegged as parents—perhaps it's because we're getting older and see life slipping through our fingers?'

Polly smiled at her. She could empathise with that! She risked a glance at Matt, but his face was impassive, his hands working deftly across Ms Harding's abdomen.

After listening with the foetal stethoscope, he gave her an old-fashioned look, and perched on the edge of the couch. 'How do you feel about going for a scan?'

'What's wrong?' she asked, her air of calm control slipping for a moment.

'Nothing—but I have a sneaking feeling you're heading for double trouble.'

'Twins?' she shrieked, and, at his nod, her head

fell back against the pillow. 'My God—I only wanted one!'

Matt chuckled. 'You may only have one—but there seem to be an awful lot of arms and legs squiggling about, and you look a bit big for twenty-four weeks.'

She groaned and dragged herself to a sitting position. 'Fantastic! What do I tell Mark?'

'How about, congratulations, darling, you're going to be a father—twice?'

She closed her eyes. 'It really should have occurred to us. He's a twin, and his father's a twin—oh, God, why me? She laughed weakly. 'That really is the pits.'

'Have the scan first before you go off the deep end,' Matt advised drily.

She left, looking bemused, and Matt and Polly finished off the clinic. The last patient was Mrs Reed, and Polly was amazed at how different she looked.

The defeated air was gone, replaced by steady determination, but she was still dreadfully thin and held together by her nerves.

As it was her first visit, Matt gave her a thorough examination, carefully keeping his face impassive.

'All seems well,' he said gently. 'You're obviously good at having babies.'

She smiled thinly, 'Without my children life wouldn't have been worth living, Dr Gregory. I just hope I don't let them down now.'

Matt gave her slender shoulders a quick hug. 'You'll be fine. We'll be keeping an eye on you and making sure you get all the help you need. If there's anything you're worried about, just give us a shout.'

After she had left, Matt turned to Polly. His eyes were angry and hard. 'Did you see her body? Covered in scars—he must have beaten her repeatedly over the years. Bastard—if I could get my hands on him——'

'Why did she stay with him so long?'

'Perhaps she was even more afraid to leave? Where would she live? I expect she was afraid they'd take her children away from her if she went, and you heard what she said about life not being worth living without them. She was caught, Polly—and thousands of women are caught in just the same way. Men, too, caught in the trap of a marriage entered into for the wrong reasons and gone painfully sour as a result. It's a trap—and for some it's a death-trap. Mrs Reed was lucky, she got out just in time, but I hope Jane and Richard don't go down the same path.'

'Oh, they won't! Matt, those two adore each other. They'll be fine.'

'I wish I had your faith, Polly,' he murmured, holding her against him for a moment.

Polly listened to his heart beating under her ear. 'I wish you did, too,' she whispered. 'I wish you did. . .'

CHAPTER SEVEN

THE next few days were busy—too busy for Polly to worry about Matt's feelings for her and his reservations about marriage. She realised that they were very serious reservations, and she just hoped that given time she could overcome them.

They weren't the only ones with problems either. Mrs Robinson came back for the rest of her well person check, and allowed Polly to do her long-overdue smear.

'How are things?' Polly asked quietly.

'Oh, you know.' Mrs Robinson smiled bleakly. 'We're trying. It isn't easy, not after so long. I can't remember the last time we sat and really talked to each other, if ever. The support group Dr Gregory referred us to is wonderful, but they can only do so much. The rest has to come from us, and it's harder than I'd realised.'

She sighed. 'Dr Gregory was right, I really don't like myself very much, but I have found out one thing—my husband loves me, for all his faults and mine. And I'm just beginning to realise that it wasn't all his fault.'

Polly smiled reassuringly. 'Sounds as if you're making progress.'

'It's just so slow, you know? I wanted a miracle——' She covered her face with her hands, and Polly let her cry for a minute before handing her a tissue. 'I know it's unrealistic, but I thought, if I could just have an operation—I know now it isn't the answer. Nothing's that easy, but I didn't think it would be this hard.' She pressed the tissue to her face, then with a visible effort she pulled herself together, blew her nose and gave Polly a wobbly smile. 'Sorry.'

'Don't be sorry. It does you good to let your feelings out. Perhaps you've held on to them for too long?'

She nodded, and Polly squeezed her hand. 'Go and do some Christmas shopping—spoil yourself a little. You'll enjoy it, and goodness knows you deserve it!'

She went out, and Matt came in a few moments later. 'Was that Mrs Robinson?'

Polly nodded, and filled him in on her progress.

'Wish I could give her an instant cure—take one of these three times a day and you'll be fine, that sort of thing.' He gave her a lop-sided grin. 'All set for tomorrow night, Pollyanna?'

'Oh, gosh, the party! I'd forgotten. Perhaps I'd better take my own advice and go shopping? I could do with something decent in my wardrobe.'

'Not too decent, I hope?' Matt teased gently. 'How about a bit of bare shoulder and the odd glimpse of thigh when you move?'

Polly smacked him laughingly on the arm. 'Behave. You're getting carried away here. High neck and ankle-length, I was thinking of.'

'How chaste—very tempting!'

Laughing, Polly pushed him through the door. 'Go away. You're damaging my concentration.'

She followed him down the corridor, and, as he

turned left towards Reception, Polly veered right
and went into the waiting-room.

'Mr Grey, would you like to come through now?'

Matt joined them in the corridor. 'Hello, Mr
Grey. Don't you think Polly would look nice in one
of those off-the-shoulder taffeta dresses?'

Polly blushed, Mr Grey chuckled and Matt
smirked unrepentantly and whistled his way cheerfully to his room.

'How are things with the great romance, then,
Polly, my dear?'

She laughed reluctantly. 'Fine, Mr Grey. Just fine.
Let's have a look at your leg, now.'

He was right, of course. Polly turned slowly in front
of the mirror. The off-the-shoulder cut was very
feminine, and the fabric clung and let go as she
moved, swaying with her body. It wasn't taffeta,
because she was too short and full-breasted for the
sort of gown he was on about. She would have felt
like an overdressed cabbage in one of them, but this
sheer silk crepe in a deep emerald-green was a
different matter altogether; with one shoulder bare
and a soft wrap-over that met at the waist and fell in
delicate pleats to the sloping hemline, it made her
feel all woman, utterly feminine and completely
desirable. She bought it, wincing slightly at the hole
it made in her bank balance but deciding it was
worth it—even if she did have to fight Matt off.

Perhaps she wouldn't bother any more? Perhaps
it was time. . .

* * *

The party was on Saturday night, at the big six-teenth-century farmhouse where Anne and Mike Haynes had made their home for the last twenty-four years. Evolution had played its part, and the old house rambled and meandered from one level to another with uninhibited delight.

Polly loved it. Her parents had owned a smaller version before they had retired to Frinton, and she had grown up in a rabbit warren of odd little rooms clustered around a large central core.

The fire in the main reception-room was blazing merrily, and soft music drifted in and out of the nooks and crannies. Everyone was in a party mood, and the heady smell of mulled wine and mince pies mingled with the scent of woodsmoke, making an intoxicating combination.

Across the room, Polly met Matt's eyes and the heat of his gaze made the fire seem cold. His eyes dropped from hers, and made a leisurely and thor-ough inspection of every inch of her. When his eyes met hers again, the message in them was far from leisurely and Polly felt heat race over her entire body. He lifted his glass in a silent toast, and drank deeply before turning back to Stephen Webster and his wife Jill.

'Polly? Yoo-hoo!' Angela waved her hand in front of Polly, and grinned when she jumped, startled. The heat of Matt's gaze spread and she flushed.

'Sorry, Angela, I was miles away.'

'Liar,' she said softly. 'You were about twenty feet away, if that. Let's go and give Anne a hand in the kitchen.'

They made their way out through the hall and

down to the huge homely kitchen, where their hostess was busy pulling mince pies and sausage rolls out of the big Aga's oven. There was a cold buffet laid in the dining-room, and snacks scattered throughout the house.

'Anything we can do?' Angela asked as they went in.

Anne lifted her immaculate head and pulled a face. 'Don't think so. I think the girls have got everything pretty much under control, thanks. Stay and have a chat. There's a jug of wine on the side— grab a glass.'

Angela propped a slender hip against the worktop and poured three glasses of mulled wine, handing one to each of them.

'Here's to you,' Anne said, and then switched her gimlet eye to Polly exclusively. 'My dear, you look most—alluring, doesn't she, Angela? Very lovely indeed. That should knock him out of his socks if nothing else does.'

Polly spluttered. 'I'm sure—Matt doesn't——'

Anne levelled a spatula at Polly and wagged it menacingly. 'What that young man wants and what he needs are two entirely different things. What he has apparently failed to realise is that he would find both of them in you. If that delightful little dress pushes him into it, all well and good. Have a mince pie.'

She slid the tray of steaming pies towards Polly. Overwhelmed and outmanoeuvred, Polly took one and munched it in silence while Angela and Anne sipped their wine and chatted about the practice

computer system which Anne, a computer consult-
ant, had helped to set up.

After a moment or two the phone rang, and
Stephen disappeared through the front door. Mike
wandered into the kitchen.

'Someone has to be on call,' he said with a shrug,
raiding the mince pies. 'At least he gets Christmas
off completely. I'm on on Boxing Day, but poor old
Matt's drawn the short straw this year. As he said,
he's the only one without family commitments, so
he might as well. Seems a bit tough—I asked him if
he'd like to come here and have Christmas lunch
with us, but he declined.'

'What are you doing for Christmas, Polly?' Anne
asked.

Polly shrugged. 'Nothing. My parents are midway
through their cruise at the moment, and my
brother's going to his wife's parents for a week, so
I'm on my own.'

Anne's eyes narrowed slightly with the light of
battle. 'Why not get together with Matt? You could
make it a lovely, cosy little Christmas with just the
two of you——'

Polly smiled slightly, uneasy with the woman's
determined matchmaking. 'I'll think about it,' she
said quietly, and jumped when a strong, firm arm
came around her waist and hugged her back against
a solid chest.

'Think about what?' Matt murmured in her ear.

'Nothing. Have a mince pie,' Polly said, desperately trying to change the subject. Stephen's wife Jill
joined them then, and they all drifted back to the
sitting-room.

They were just passing the dining-room when Mike and Anne's nineteen-year-old daughter Rebecca came flying out, laughing, with a young man hard on her heels.

They cannoned into the cluster of people, and a handbag was knocked off the table and fell to the floor, disgorging its contents all over the carpet.

'Oh, no!' Rebecca said, and knelt down, grabbing things and stuffing them back in. Polly and Matt also crouched down to retrieve the things, and as they straightened, Matt spotted something else.

'Here,' he said, a packet of contraceptive pills held between finger and thumb.

Polly looked up and caught Rebecca's anguished glance, conscious of Mike's indrawn breath and everyone's attention.

'Thank you,' she mumbled, and, taking the bag from Rebecca, she snatched the pills from Matt's fingers and pushed them into the bag. She could feel her cheeks flaming, but the tension in the air around them dissolved instantly.

Mike and Anne exchanged knowing glances, Matt looked puzzled, but Rebecca and her boyfriend just looked relieved.

'Thanks,' Rebecca muttered a moment later, and Polly smiled weakly.

'It's OK. They all think Matt and I—well, no one would be surprised.'

'But won't Matt know?'

'I'll deal with him. Don't worry.'

Stephen rejoined them a short while later and they gravitated to the dining-room for supper. When they had all eaten their fill, Mike handed over control of

the music to Rebecca's boyfriend, dimmed the lights
and swept Anne into his arms. Stephen and Jill
joined them, followed by Angela and Bob. The
music was romantic, the mood unashamedly sentimental. Polly ached.

Matt appeared at her side, his eyes warm. 'Would
you like to dance?' he asked softly.

She nodded, suddenly breathless. He held out his
arms, and she went into them with a wonderful sense
of homecoming. She felt his shoulder beneath her
cheek, his hands warm and firm against her spine.

His breath moved against her hair, teasing her
senses. 'I've wanted to do this all night,' he whispered, and urged her closer. His lips were against
her hair, and a muffled groan came from them as
their thighs chafed gently together. 'Polly, have you
any idea how beautiful you look tonight?'

Polly had been pleased with her appearance, but
she hadn't really expected to hear the note of awe in
his voice. It left her speechless. She hugged him
instead, and all that did was bring their bodies even
closer together.

'God, let's get out of here,' he whispered rag-
gedly, and drew her out into the hall, pausing there
to kiss her thoroughly before picking up her coat
from the settle and draping it round her shoulders.
Then he pulled on his own overcoat, stuck his head
round the door and waggled his fingers to Mike. Just
then Anne rounded the corner.

'I'm taking Polly home,' Matt said casually.

'Not before time,' Anne retorted, and leant up to
kiss his cheek. As she leant towards Polly to kiss
her, she winked broadly, and Polly blushed.

The journey back was silent, filled with tension. Polly was sure by now that Matt was expecting to make love to her, and she didn't know if she had the self-will or determination to stop him, but she still wasn't sure it was right for them yet.

'We'll go to my place,' he said eventually, 'Taffy will need to be let out.'

'No. Take me home, Matt, please,' she said quietly.

'What?' He braked and pulled the car over into a lay-by. 'Polly, I don't understand.'

She closed her eyes and pressed her fingers to her brow. 'Matt, it's too soon. I don't think you're ready——'

He grabbed her hand and ground it firmly against his lap. 'Are you joking? How ready do I have to be?'

Gently, reluctantly, she eased her fingers from his grasp and pulled her hand away.

'That isn't what I meant, Matt.'

He groaned, and brought his fist down on the steering-wheel. 'Polly, I want you—I need you. You need me, too. How long are you going to do this to us?'

'For as long as it takes,' she replied quietly. Her voice was shaking, and tears were filling her eyes. 'I love you, Matt, you know that. But there are things between us that shouldn't be there.'

'Such as what? Clothes?'

She ignored the heavy sarcasm in his tone. 'The spectre of your marriage, for a start. All that bitterness—you won't give us a chance, Matt. Oh, yes,

you want to take me to bed—but to make love to
me, or to—hell, I can't even say it, it's so awful.'

'To screw you,' he said flatly.

She flinched. 'Yes.'

There was a long, impenetrable silence, then Matt
sighed deeply.

'I'll take you home, Polly. I can't be what you
want. I'm sorry.'

Polly bit her lip and tried to stop the tears, but
they flooded down her cheeks. She held back the
sobs, though, until Matt turned into her drive,
opened the door and helped her out. As he tipped
up her face to kiss her goodnight, he saw the tears
falling down her pale cheeks and his face contracted
in pain.

'Oh, Polly, darling, don't! I want to love you,' he
groaned, and held her hard against his chest, rocking
her as she sobbed her heart out. 'Darling, I'm sorry.
Don't cry. Oh, Polly, what have I done to you?'

'It's not your fault,' she said with a sniff, and lifted
her tear-stained face to him. 'Come and have a
coffee.'

Then went in together, and while Polly made the
coffee Matt tended to the fire.

'Did I ever thank you for that fire?' she asked,
coming in with the tray.

'Several times. Here, let me take that.'

He put the tray down on the table, and sitting in a
chair, he tugged Polly down on to his lap. He had
taken off his glasses, and his tie was loosened, the
top button gaping to show a soft curl of chest hair at
his throat. Polly longed to ease off the rest of his
shirt and bury her fingers in the curls.

'Did you mean what you said?' she asked him after a minute. 'About wanting to love me?'

He sighed and let his head fall back. 'Yes, I meant it. Life would be so simple if I could just allow myself the myth of happy endings. Of course I want to love you. You're a wonderful girl—who wouldn't want to love you? You're warm, generous, kind, thoughtful, responsive, beautiful—God only knows what you see in me.'

'Oh, you're warm, generous, kind, thoughtful, beautiful—have I left anything out?'

Matt laughed, a deep rumble in his chest that sent tremors through Polly's side. 'Responsive, and men are not beautiful.'

'You are,' Polly said seriously, her soft brown eyes meshing with the steel blue of his.

'Oh, Polly——' He broke off, unable to speak as the desire flowed between them like a river of molten lava.

'Certainly responsive,' she whispered 'Fancy leaving that one out.'

He rocked his hips against her. 'Fancy,' he breathed. 'Oh, God, Polly, I want you——' He brought his lips down tenderly on hers, and she arched against him, drowning in sensation. 'Polly, I—it would be making love, not—you mean an awful lot to me. I think I do love you, as much as I can love anyone. But it isn't enough, and I daren't let it be more. I'm afraid, Polly.'

She took his face between her hands and held it tenderly, meeting his eyes with all the love in her own. 'I'll never hurt you, Matt. Surely you know that?'

He moved away from her, distancing himself both physically and mentally. 'You can't say that. You can't make those sort of hollow promises. Look, I'm very tempted to say I love you so you'll let me make love to you. In just the same way, I think you feel if you can make me trust you, then I'll be able to love you, *ergo* we can go to bed. The outcome is the same, and the motive is the same. We're adults, Polly, healthy sexual adults. It isn't wrong. What is wrong is all these damn silly games people have to play to justify their hormones!'

Polly was hurt. 'I'm not playing games, Matt, and I never said it was wrong for us to make love, just wrong for us now, at this time. And you're right, I do want you. I'd like nothing more than to let you make love to me, but it wouldn't help us. Matt, I've only had one affair, with a man who was very fond of me but didn't really love me. I didn't love him either, and yet when he went away I was desolate. Matt, I would *die* without you now. If you'd made love to me as well—Matt, I really don't think I could survive.'

He was silent for a long while, staring into the flames, then he lifted his head and rested it against hers, holding her close.

'You'd survive.' He pressed his lips to her hair, and said softly, 'Elaine was a bitch. She thought she wanted to be married to a doctor, so she allowed herself to get pregnant. I had just done my finals and was starting my house year. Her timing was atrocious. I was working on average ninety hours a week, on call for over a hundred. After three months of living with a shadow she decided it was time to take matters into her own hands. During the day she started seeing this man—I knew nothing about it, but our sex life was non-existent and I put it down to her pregnancy. To be honest, I was so tired I was relieved. Then I was scheduled to be on call over Christmas and she decided she wasn't going to stay around our flat on her own. She and her boyfriend booked a holiday in the Canaries, and she told me she was going to stay with her parents.

'I knew nothing about it until I got a call in broken English telling me that my wife had had a waterskiing accident and that she had lost the baby. She was was five months pregnant.'

He paused, and his face reflected his anguish. Polly waited in silence while he struggled for control, then he went on, his voice a little rough, 'She came home on her own, and for a few weeks she was very subdued, but then I think reality set in and she realised what she'd done. Naturally, she found it hard to take. She started to party, and again I knew nothing about it because I was so tired I was useless. I let her down, I suppose, by not being there for her, but she didn't seem to want me when I was, and life was rough enough without taking any extra hassle on board. I think I wanted to punish her, because deep down I couldn't forgive her for what she'd done to my baby. So I let it slide.'

'In the end she went to a party, and she told a friend there that she'd left me and was going to this other man. She left the party at about two-thirty, and at six in the morning they brought her into Casualty. They'd fished her out of the river—her car had run off the road and she'd drowned. They wanted a doctor to certify her death.'

'Oh, Matt!' Polly slipped her arms around him and hugged him tight, and he returned the hug.

'I just felt numb. I told them they'd have to get someone else to certify her, but I could identify her for them. They called the registrar down from surgical and he took me home and put me to bed.'

Polly was horrified. 'How did you cope?'

He shrugged. 'I didn't. I came unglued for a while, but then I moved out of the flat and into residence, and threw myself into work for the next two years. By the time I came up for air, I was over her. To be honest, I don't think it took that long. We hardly spent any time together, and if it hadn't been for the baby we would never have got married. The baby, though—that's a different story. I don't think I'll ever really get over it.'

'Oh, darling, I'm so sorry. . .'

He gave her a level look. 'I don't need your pity, Polly, I've got that pain under control, where I can handle it. I really can't talk about it, so don't ask me to. In any case, it's nothing to do with us.'

He released Polly pointedly, and she stood up. 'The coffee's cold. I'll make some more.'

'Don't bother. I'm going home, Polly. I'm not very good company at the moment.'

He kissed her briefly, gave her a smile that didn't reach his eyes, and left.

So now she knew. She watched the lights on his car as he reversed out into the lane and drove off, but he didn't look back.

What had she achieved by all that heart-searching? Nothing, except to upset him and drive him away. She felt further from him tonight than she had ever felt in all the six weeks she had known him, and for the first time she felt that it was hopeless.

How could you save someone from himself when he didn't want to be saved?

On a wave of misery, Polly threw out the cold coffee, locked up the cottage and trailed up to bed, alone again.

So she had still preserved her beloved principles. So what? She could even now have been lying in his arms, enjoying the warmth of his love—because he did love her, even though he wouldn't admit it. Polly picked up her old raggedy teddy bear and cuddled him.

'What should I do, Bear? If I get another chance, I'll take it. I don't think anything could hurt more than this, and at least we would have had something to remember. If only he would take a chance too. . .'

CHAPTER EIGHT

POLLY didn't see Matt on Sunday. She didn't really expect to, but it was the first Sunday for weeks she had spent totally on her own, and she missed his company unbearably.

Except for the weekends when he had been on call, they had been together for most of the day, walking the dog, going for drives or just simply working on Matt's cottage.

Polly had helped him with his bedroom, stripping off umpteen layers of wallpaper and helping him to repair the plaster prior to painting. It had been unbelievably messy and very homely, punctuated by kisses and cups of tea, and they found that they worked well together.

So this particular Sunday was just a yawning void, and as the day wore into evening Polly lost the slim hope she had resurrected so briefly the night before.

She went to bed early, willing the phone to ring, and lay awake until the small hours before falling finally into a restless sleep.

Monday was hectic. She saw Matt only briefly before his ante-natal clinic, and their communication during the afternoon was strictly professional.

He shot out of the surgery just before his last patient, handing her over to Mike Haynes as he had to go out on call and would be some considerable time. He was on call for the night, and Polly knew she wouldn't see him.

The only time she was likely to be able to see him, in fact, was Christmas Day itself, which was Wednesday. Anne Haynes' idea of a nice, cosy Christmas together seemed a million miles away— unless. . .? Polly dragged on her warm clothes and went to Longridge's only supermarket, which was open late in the few days before Christmas.

Hoping she was doing the right thing, she loaded her trolley and headed home.

Tuesday was no better. It was Christmas Eve, but the surgery was running as normal up until seven, disposing of as many problems as possible before the Christmas break.

By the end of the day Polly felt like a hit-and-run victim. She went home, sorted out her mail and stood up some Christmas cards. Then she sat down on the floor in front of the fire and wrapped a present, putting it and various other things in the boot of her car before making a drink and going up to bed.

Just before midnight she heard the church bells, and as she was still wide awake she slipped out of bed, wrapped up warmly and went to Midnight Mass.

It was a choral service, and it had just started when Polly slipped inside the back of the church. Head down, she made her way to the nearest pew and squeezed in on the end. The carols were lovely, reminding Polly of family Christmases and days spent on duty on the wards during her training. They

brought a lump to her throat, and she shut her eyes
to stop the tears that squeezed past her lids.

Someone pushed a clean handkerchief into her
clenched hands, and she blotted her eyes and looked
up to see Matt beside her. She looked quickly away,
torn by a pain she couldn't deal with.

His hand found hers, and slowly his warmth and
comfort flowed into her. With it came her hope,
restored bit by bit as the service went on. Gradually
she settled down and began to join in, enjoying the
sound of Matt's warm baritone mingling with her
own clear, lilting tones.

As they left the church after the service, they saw
the Haynes family in the churchyard on the way out.

'Over to you, dear boy,' said Mike, and handed
Matt the cell-phone. 'Give me a buzz if you can't
cope.'

Matt nodded. 'Will do. Happy Christmas.'

They shook hands, and Anne kissed Matt and
then Polly, whispering in her ear, 'Now remember
what I said!'

Polly smiled. 'I have,' she returned softly.

They left the Haynes family deep in conversation
with other members of the congregation, and made
their way steadily towards the gate, exchanging
greetings and handshakes with several patients on
the way down the path.

Eventually they arrived at Polly's car. Her heart
in her throat, Polly turned to Matt.

'Here we are.'

He looked down at her in silence for a moment,
then cupped her shoulders gently in his hands.

'Happy Christmas, Polly,' he murmured, and low-ered his lips to hers for a fleeting kiss.

Then he turned on his heel and left, striding away down the street, his breath misting on the cold air as he called greetings to his patients.

Polly let herself into her car and drove wearily home, assailed by doubts.

In the morning, she woke bright and early and dressed carefully in a fine black wool skirt, sparkly tights and long boots. Her favourite mohair jumper with the appliqué topped the outfit, and she clipped her hair back with two tortoiseshell slides. Pulling on her coat, she loaded everything into her car, banked the fire and set off, her heart in her mouth.

What would he say?

She arrived at the cottage just as he was pulling out.

'Hi!' she called.

He cut the engine. 'What brings you here?' he asked, not altogether welcoming.

Polly forcibly kept her expression cheerful. 'I've come to see Taffy. I knew you wouldn't be able to take him for a walk today, so I thought I'd do it. Could you let me have a key so I can let him back in if you aren't here when we get back?'

He turned off the ignition, went back into the house and emerged a moment later with a spare key.

'Here. Just leave it on the kitchen table. Thanks, Polly.'

Their hands touched as she took the key, and she jumped as if she'd been scalded.

Matt paused, as if he wanted to say something else, and then he shook his head. 'Must get on. If you hang on for me, I'm going up to see Mrs Reed later if I get ten seconds. Care to come?'

'Love to,' she said, with her first genuine smile of the morning, and she waved as he drove off.

Her conscience pricking her for using him, she changed into her wellies and took the wretched dog for a walk over the fields behind Matt's house. He had just returned by the time they got back, so she changed back to her boots and climbed into his car while he waited on the drive.

'What's wrong with Mrs Reed?' Polly asked.

Matt grinned. 'Nothing. I've been given so many bottles of sherry and Irish Cream and boxes of chocolates that I'll be an alcoholic and a diabetic by the time I've fought my way through them. I thought she could probably find a use for them.'

Polly eyed him. 'Is that the truth?'

He laughed. 'Not entirely, but it'll do!'

They drew up outside Mrs Reed's house, and Matt helped Polly out, then handed her an armful of chocolate boxes.

Together they walked up the path and knocked on the front door.

There was a babble and tumbling from the other side of the door, and then two laughing children wrenched the door open. Mrs Reed appeared at the back of the hall surrounded by the other children, and her hand flew to her mouth with surprise.

'Hello, Doctor! Fancy seeing you—and the nurse! Come in—gracious, we're in a bit of a mess, but do come in—Sammy, clear that chair for the nurse. David, get that cat off the settee and move up a bit.'

Matt stopped her flustered movements by taking

hold of her shoulders and kissing her firmly on the cheek. 'Happy Christmas, Mrs Reed. Listen, we aren't here to hold up your celebrations, but I wonder if you could do me a favour? My patients have been as generous as usual, and I'm overloaded with chocolates and things like that. I daren't hurt their feelings, but I can't possibly get through them all and I haven't got any family to hand any of them on to. I wondered if your brood could manage to find a home for some of them?'

'Oh, Dr Gregory!' Her eyes filled, and she gave him a wobbly smile. 'I'm sure they could. Mr Fairchild, Richard's boss, gave us a turkey, and old Mr Grey gave me some sprouts out of the garden, and now this—they can have a proper Christmas. . .'

She turned away, hand pressed to her mouth, and Matt gave her a brief hug. 'If I'd known it would make you cry, I'd have hung on to them!' he joked softly, and she gave a little hiccuping laugh.

'You're a good man.'

'Rubbish. I'm just human. Here, do you think you could hand on this lot to Jane and Richard? Sort of a housewarming.'

She nodded. 'I'll do that. They're coming round soon—in fact, we thought you might have been them, but I expect the babe's holding them up.'

They chatted for a few more minutes, and then left. As they were driving back through the town, the cell-phone buzzed. Polly answered it while Matt pulled over, then she handed him the phone.

'Right, I'm on my way. I'll be with you in five minutes, Mr Pennington. Try to keep her calm.' He switched off the phone and turned to Polly. 'Elderly woman with what sounds like a heart attack. Can you manage to walk back to your car from here? They're just round the corner.'

'Sure.' Polly jumped out of the car and waved as he pulled out and roared away. It was only a few minutes to the cottage, and she still had his key in her pocket.

Her heart lighter now, she walked briskly back to the cottage and let herself in. After shutting Taffy in the kitchen, she went out to her car and unloaded several bags and boxes from the boot. Some she took into the kitchen, the others into the sitting-room.

She started in the kitchen first. Rooting around in Matt's cupboards, she found a roasting tin and placed the little turkey breast roast in the centre, surrounded it with sausages wrapped in bacon and a few potatoes which she peeled quickly, and stood it in the middle of the table. She tipped the bag of frozen sprouts into a pan, put the cream and the Christmas pudding in the fridge and leaving the rest of the trimmings in the box, went through to the sitting-room.

It was, as usual, warm, clean and tidy, but apart from several Christmas cards in a pile on the side there was no attempt at decoration. It could have been any day of the year, and it offended Polly's sentimental soul. Opening a long, thin box, she pulled out a little artificial tree and opened out its branches, then stood it on a table by the window and draped fairy lights over it. By the time she had hung a few baubles on it and switched on the lights, it looked very pretty, and she set up the Christmas cards on the dresser and around the window sills as a finishing touch.

She was hanging the little holly and ribbon wreath on the front door when Matt turned into the drive.

He stepped out of the car in silence, and his eyes went from her to the sitting-room window where the fairy lights twinkled bravely, and then back to her again. They were quite expressionless.

With a sinking heart, Polly fastened the bow and turned to face him.

'Hello, Matt. How was Mrs Pennington?'

'I've admitted her. She'll be all right, I think. Polly, what the hell are you up to?'

'It's a surprise,' she began, but his harsh bark of laughter cut her off.

'I'll say it's a surprise!' He pushed past her into the sitting-room, and stood staring at the little tree with its cluster of presents underneath, and the cards arranged all round the room, and then he shut his eyes and tugged off his glasses, tucking them into his top pocket.

'I'm sorry the tree's only artificial, but there wasn't time to get a real one——'

'Polly, what the hell is all this in aid of?'

'In aid of? What do you mean, what's it in aid of? Christmas, for heaven's sake!'

He sighed. 'Polly, I'm sure you mean well, but I really could do without all this today. I'm busy, I'm on call, it's been a rough night and it promises to get worse. I don't *want* all these tidings of comfort and joy!'

He marched into the kitchen, and slammed to a halt. Polly cannoned into his back.

'Damn, damn and double bloody damn——'

'Don't swear, Matt! It's Christmas!'

'I don't care what bloody day it is, Polly, I *don't want to know*!'

Polly blinked back the tears. 'Suit yourself, though why you should think Mrs Reed needs presents and cheering up on Christmas Day and yet you don't is beyond me. As you told her, you are human—you could try acting it!'

She turned on her heel and snatched up her coat from the banisters, just as the phone started to ring.

'What am I supposed to do with all this lot?'

'Put it in the bin, if you really feel so strongly about it. Answer the phone first. Goodbye, Matt.'

'Polly, wait—hello, Dr Gregory here. Mr Goddard—fine, get the packs out, put a plastic sheet on the bed and hang on. We're on our way. Call the midwife—she's out? OK. I'll bring the practice nurse. See you in a tick.'

He replaced the receiver. 'Did you hear?'

She nodded numbly. 'Do you need me?'

He looked at her for a long moment, then closed his eyes. 'Yes, Polly, I need you. Will you forgive me for long enough to come? This baby won't wait.'

'Then let's go.'

They headed out of the door together, and made good time to the Goddard's house on the outskirts of town. The oldest child, a boy of six, opened the door.

'Mum's having the baby,' he said.

Matt grinned. 'Yes, we know. That's why we're here. May we come in?'

He nodded, and they went quickly in to the warm hall.

'Mr Goddard? We're here,' Matt called, and a head stuck itself over the banisters.

'Hi. Come on up. She's pushing.'

'Good grief!' Polly said, and Matt laughed.

'She knows how to do it,' he said over his shoulder, and Polly followed him up the stairs, their row forgotten.

When they entered the bedroom, it was obvious that Mrs Goddard's labour was well advanced. She was sitting propped up on the pillows, her nightie hitched up round her hips, and she was pushing steadily.

As the contraction faded she opened her eyes, lifted her head and grinned weakly at Matt.

'You told me not to do too much, didn't you?'

'What were you up to?' Matt asked, rolling up his sleeves and washing his hands at the basin.

She shrugged eloquently. 'Getting the Christmas dinner. Nothing much——'

Matt laughed. 'Is it in the oven?'

'Yup. I nearly didn't make it, but it's in, and the sprouts are peeled, and the Christmas pudding's steaming—all set. It'll be ready in an hour or so. I thought we'd be ready by then!'

Another contraction gripped her, and Matt perched on the bed and listened to the baby's heartbeat. As the contraction passed, he pulled on his gloves and turned back to Mrs Goddard.

'OK, let's have a look and see how you're doing.'

As Polly watched, he examined Mrs Goddard

quickly and efficiently, a smile spreading over his face as he did so.

'You don't believe in giving us much time, do you?' he chuckled. 'Get your skates on, Polly, this baby is coming now!'

Scrubbing up quickly, she opened the pack and pulled on the plastic apron, then the gloves.

As she prepared the sutures, the swabs and the chlorhexidine solution, Matt was opening the obstetric bag kept at the practice and getting out the episiotomy scissors and the suction tube for the baby.

All the time he was working, he kept up a running gag with Tim and Sarah Goddard, and Polly marvelled at his cool. As he slipped on the gloves and straightened, Polly saw him close his eyes as if to compose himself.

Then the competent professional was back, calm and efficient, issuing relaxed instructions at the speed of light. Tim was stationed at Sarah's side, supporting her legs, and Polly was to make sure he got the correct implements at the correct time if necessary. She was remembering why she hadn't gone in for midwifery when Sarah groaned.

'Here comes another contraction,' she said, and Tim held her hand while she panted her way through it. 'I want to push!' she muttered through clenched teeth, and Matt grinned.

'Tough!' he said. 'Just keep right on panting, lady. You can push when I say so and not before.'

He winked at Polly. 'Right, let's get this little bundle out into the world, shall we?'

Carefully supporting her perineum with the thumb

and forefinger of one hand, he used the other to lift the baby's head slightly and ease it out as the contraction passed. Immediately Matt took Sarah's hand and laid it on the baby's head, and her face lit up.

'Cord's round the neck,' Matt said to Polly in an undertone. 'Can you get the artery forceps and scissors handy just in case I can't shift it?' He slipped his finger under the cord and wriggled a loop free, then slipped it easily over the baby's head.

'Damn, it's round twice!' he muttered.

'There's another one coming,' Sarah warned him, and Matt swore softly.

'Just hang on as long as you can, I'm nearly there.'

Polly could see the beads of sweat standing out on his brow, but his hands were steady as he eased the cord gently round.

'Got it!' he said with a sigh, and Sarah moaned.

'I have to push—I've got to!'

'Come on, then,' Matt said gently, 'nice and steady.'

She gave one last push, and immediately Matt lifted the baby clear and held it upside down to drain the passages.

'It's a girl,' Sarah cried, and Tim hugged her.

'Suck her out, Polly, let's get her breathing,' Matt said calmly, and when Polly had sucked out her mouth and upper respiratory tract he laid her over Sarah's tummy and flicked the soles of her feet gently with his fingers. Within seconds she had let out a bellow of rage, her face screwed up and purple with effort, and a bright pink flush spread over her tiny body. Matt sank back on to his heels and grinned. 'Good girl!' he said, and handed her to her delighted mother. 'Here you go—happy Christmas, Sarah.'

Matt injected her thigh with Syntometrine. 'Better late than never,' he said with a chuckle, and Polly marvelled at his cool. She felt weak with relief, giddy with happiness and unbearably lonely. On top of Matt's reaction to her Christmas surprise, it was the last straw.

She turned away and busied herself with the sutures while she got her feelings back under control. Matt was busy delivering and checking the placenta while Tim bathed the baby and Sarah panicked about the Christmas lunch.

'Polly, would you like to go and turn off the oven so this woman relaxes, please? Oh, and you might make sure the children are still in one piece.'

'They are. We would have heard the screams. I think Tim left them with a tin of Quality Street.'

Matt chuckled. 'Thought they were quiet!'

'Actually,' Tim said seriously, trying very hard to look hurt, 'our next door neighbour is with them, and there's no need for Polly to be banished to the kitchen. There's a bottle of champagne over there, Polly, and four glasses. Would you like to cuddle this little beast while I see if I can get it open?'

He popped the cork and poured a splash in each glass, then handed them round.

'Congratulations'

'Many thanks!'

'Bless you!'

'Well done!'

There was a clash of glasses, and they all drank to

the baby's health. They were standing around laughing heartily when a woman popped her head round the door.

'Did we hear a baby cry?' she asked.

'You did indeed,' Tim said proudly, and took the new baby down to see her little brothers and sister.

In no time Matt and Polly had cleared up, the mother and baby were setttled down and the rest of the family were talking about Christmas lunch.

'Won't you stay and join us?' Tim said, but Matt shook his head.

'We've got our own at home, waiting to go in the oven. We'll leave you in peace. I'll pop back later on, and I expect the midwife will be in to see you later too. Anything out of the ordinary, ring me. I'll come straight over.'

They left amid a hail of thanks and good wishes, and Polly leant back against the car seat and sighed.

'Tired?'

She rolled her head towards him. 'No, not really. Just shell-shocked. I panicked a bit about the cord. You were marvellous.'

'It was a very easy delivery. She's the ideal candidate for home birth.'

Matt swung the car into the drive, and as they went in through the front door, he pulled Polly into his arms.

'Polly, I'm sorry about what I said before. I know you were only trying to be kind, and I just over-reacted. Will you forgive me?'

'It's my fault,' she mumbled into his shirt, 'I shouldn't just assume everybody wants to be happy all the time. It's a great fault I have, that I expect everyone to wear a huge smile from when they get out of bed to when they fall back in it. I have to learn to respect people's wishes—and sometimes I just need telling a bit hard.'

'Not that hard,' he whispered, and tipping up her head, he kissed her gently. 'I always seem to hurt you—I don't mean to.'

He kissed her again, then dropping his arm around her shoulders, he led her into the kitchen.

'Oh, my God!'

Polly looked up, and groaned. 'Oh, no! Matt, why didn't I *think*? Oh, Taffy, you naughty dog!'

Taffy, replete but guilt-ridden, squirmed across the floor to their feet and rolled disarmingly on to his back.

'Stop the disgusting behaviour, you reprehensible hound! Out!' Matt marched over to the door and yanked it open, and a chastened Taffy scuttled out into the garden. 'Here,' Matt yelled, throwing a piece of sausage after him, 'you missed a bit! Damn dog!' He turned back to Polly, a smile on his face, but she had sagged against the table, hands over her face, and her shoulders were shaking.

'Ah, Polly love, don't cry. It was a lovely thought, but it doesn't matter. Come on.'

A chuckle escaped her, and Matt pulled down her hands and scowled at her. 'I thought you were crying!'

In answer she opened her arms, and he moved into them, hugging her and laughing.

Then together, they cleaned up the mess Taffy had left, threw together some sandwiches and went into the sitting-room. Matt relented enough to let

Taffy back in, but he wisely stayed out of the way in his bed.

After they had eaten, Matt went up and had a shower and changed, and then Polly handed him his presents.

'Oh, Polly. . .' He opened the flat squashy one first. 'Gloves! Polly, they're lovely—how did you know I needed new gloves?'

She smiled. 'I saw one of them in Taffy's bed the other day.'

The other present was an old key, a heavy black iron one with an ornate ring. It would go with his collection on the bressumer over the fire, she had thought.

'It's just right—thank you. I needed one more to balance things.'

'I know you did. That's why I've given it to you— it's the key to my heart,' she said softly.

'But not your chastity belt?' he joked, but his eyes were serious, searching.

'They go together,' Polly told him, never taking her eyes from his.

'Are you sure you want me to have it?' he asked, and his voice had a slight tremor of vulnerability that Polly had never heard before.

'Quite sure,' she said. 'I trust you with it.'

'God, Polly—I can't guarantee you a happy ending, darling.'

Polly shrugged. 'I'll take whatever you can give me—however much or little. I love you.'

The silence stretched on for a breathless moment. 'Polly——'

The phone rang, shattering the silence.

'Get it,' Polly murmured.

'What timing,' he said gruffly, reaching for the receiver. 'Dr Gregory here.'

Polly watched as he scribbled down an address and handed Polly the phone number of the cell-phone.

'Do you need me?'

He grinned. 'Are we back to that again?'

She blushed, and he dropped a quick kiss on her brow. 'Stay here. I'll be as quick as possible. Could you get the phone and refer anyone who sounds urgent?'

She nodded. 'Shall I get us something to eat later?' she called after him.

'Lovely. I'll be back as soon as I can.'

She watched him go, and wondered what she had done. Too late to turn back now, though. Humming softly to herself, she went into the kitchen and prepared a casserole, then ran lightly upstairs and showered, dressing again and making up her face with care.

She laid the table in the kitchen and stood a red candle in the centre, with a twist of ivy round the base, and opened the bottle of red wine to breathe.

Then she settled down in the sitting-room to wait for him.

CHAPTER NINE

IT WAS dark when Matt let himself back in. There was a delicious smell coming from the kitchen, and Taffy padded up to him, wagging his plumy tail and smiling his welcome.

'Hello, you bad dog,' Matt said softly, fondling his ears, and then went in search of Polly. He found her in the sitting-room, curled up on the settee asleep. It was dark in there except for the fairy lights, and she looked unbelievably tiny melting into the shadows.

He went quietly back into the kitchen and stood staring at the beautifully laid table in the centre of the room. His face troubled, he moved the casserole down to the bottom oven to keep warm, and then paused on his way back. The key she had given him was in his pocket where he had slipped it on his way out, and he curled his fingers round it thoughtfully.

Like Polly, it seemed to radiate warmth. The key to her heart, she had said, but was she right to trust him? It would be so easy now to slip into a much deeper relationship, but could *he* take it? And did he dare? For a moment he hesitated, then with a shaky sigh he walked slowly into the dimly lit room. He had nothing left to lose.

Polly came awake slowly. She hadn't meant to fall asleep, and now she was stiff and cramped from her awkward position. She shifted slightly and winced.

'Hi.'

She straightened up. 'Matt—I didn't hear you come in. The casserole——'

'It's fine. I've put it in the bottom oven. Are you OK?' His voice was warm and husky, and he was looking at her with a curiously tender expression.

She found her voice. 'Mmm. Bit stiff. My legs have gone to sleep——'

'Here, let me.' He shifted closer to her and his large, warm hand closed over her leg and massaged it gently, working from her ankle upwards to her thigh; then he switched to the other one.

'Better?' he murmured.

Polly lifted her eyes to his. What had started out as a simple massage had turned into a sensual caress, and she felt shaken. She hadn't realised that her legs were so sensitive, but his touch had turned her veins to rivers of fire, and the fire had spread throughout her body, burning away the last remnants of her doubt.

She smiled, a slight parting of her lips that made Matt catch his breath. He drew her into his arms and kissed her, and Polly sank against him, surrendering to his tender touch.

After an age he raised his head and stared deep into her eyes, and the love she saw there made her heart sing.

'Let me make love to you, Polly,' he murmured, his voice gruff with need.

Polly eased away from him. 'No——'

'What?' Matt's disbelief was a breathless groan, and she rose calmly to her feet.

'Not here, not like this. Come——'

Holding out her hand, she watched the disbelief replaced by hope and then passion, swift and hot, darkening his eyes and making his chest rise and fall unsteadily.

Taking her hand, he stood and followed her upstairs to his room. The lamp was lit, and a last red rose from the garden lay on the pillow.

In the golden spill of light from the hall, Polly paused and released him, then with shaking fingers she lifted the combs from her hair and laid them on the bedside table. Catching the hem of her mohair sweater, she lifted it over her head and dropped it behind her on the chair. Her skirt followed, falling softly to the floor as she released the button, and then she straightened, her heart pounding. She felt a flush creep over her skin as she stood there shyly, an ivory silk teddy draping faithfully over her curves, outlining the soft fullness of her breasts and the gentle swell of her hips.

Matt closed his eyes and opened them again, shaking his head slightly as if to clear it. 'Dear God, you're beautiful. . .'

'Your turn,' she murmured, her voice husky.

His eyes locked with hers, he unbuttoned his shirt slowly, impeded by his trembling fingers. 'Damn thing,' he muttered, and wrenched it over his head, throwing it to one side. Polly heard a rip, and a laugh bubbled up in her throat, to catch there as he turned back to her and the light flooded over him, gilding his sleek muscles and highlighting the shadowy curls across his chest.

His hands dropped to his belt, fumbling with the buckle for a second before releasing it; his zip inched down with agonising slowness, and then he hooked his thumbs in the waistband and stripped off the rest of his clothes in one.

As he straightened, Polly felt her heart thundering in her chest. He was so big compared to her, so strong and vital and undeniably, beautifully male. He held out his hand, and she reached up and took it, their fingers meshing as he drew her against him.

Wordlessly he pulled back the quilt and moved the rose, staring at it for a moment before laying it on the table. Then he turned to Polly and lifted his hand to her shoulder. With one finger he eased aside the slivers of silk that held up the teddy, and then his hands followed it down, gliding it over her hips till it fell in a sensuous shiver to the floor.

Then he lifted Polly in his arms, cradling her against his deep chest as he rested one knee on the bed and laid her tenderly down.

'Are you sure?' he whispered.

'Dear God, how can you ask? I love you Matt. . .'

With a shattered groan he stretched out beside her, gathering her to his chest and holding her tight. Then he released her, freeing his hands to trace slow circles on her skin. His mouth sought hers, and their lips clung, fanning the heat that rose between them.

He eased over her, his body trembling with desperate control, and his voice was a ragged whisper.

'Look at me, Polly,' he commanded, and then he entered her, so carefully, so tenderly that Polly's eyes flooded with tears.

'Matt!' she breathed, but her breath caught in her throat and turned to a sob of need. She arched against him, shattering the last vestige of his control, and he drove into her, the rhythm mounting until Polly thought she would die.

Then she felt the world fall away, the only reality the man in her arms, his sweat-slicked skin hot under her palms, his eyes locked with hers, burning with passion for her.

'Hold me,' she sobbed, and with a great cry he fell against her, his body shuddering beneath her hands.

'I love you, Polly,' he whispered brokenly, and she clung to him, tears spilling from her eyes.

Thank God—oh, thank God!

Gradually their breathing steadied, and he eased away from her.

'I'm too heavy for you, I'll crush you,' he murmured, but she hung on to him.

'Don't leave me,' she whispered, and he shifted to his side, holding her against him.

'OK?'

She nodded.

His hand came up and brushed away the tears that lingered on her cheeks. He looked so unbearably vulnerable, so tender. She longed to ask him if he had meant it when he had said he loved her, but she was too afraid that he would back down. She knew the admission had been torn from him, and she couldn't bear it if he denied it now.

'You're so tiny—did I hurt you?'

She shook her head. 'It was wonderful. You were wonderful.'

He grinned self-consciously. 'You were pretty wonderful yourself,' he murmured. 'I was afraid I'd be too quick for you—I couldn't hold back any longer.'

'Neither could I—why did we wait so long?'

He groaned and closed his eyes, and she chuckled.

They lay like that for some time, letting the sensations die away and reality return. Then Matt sighed. 'I'm starving, but I can't be bothered to get up.'

'Lazy-bones!' she teased.

'Huh! And just who was it curled up on the settee asleep? Hmm? Hmm?' He prodded her in the ribs, and she giggled.

There was a playful glint in his eye, and his hand came up to cup her breast just as the phone rang.

He groaned and flopped back on the pillow. 'Answer it—tell them I've gone to Mars for the holidays and Dr Haynes is on call.'

Polly reached out for the phone. 'Hello, Dr Gregory's house. Just a moment, please, I'll get him.'

She handed him the phone and swatted his hand off her breast. It landed on her thigh, and he ran it firmly upwards.

'Dr Gregory speaking. What can I do for you?'

His hand teased the curls at the apex of her thighs, and she rolled away. He followed her. 'I'll be with you in about half an hour,' he said finally, and there was a moment of silence before he added, 'Well, I could be quicker, but it's unlikely—in fact it may take longer. I have to make love to my girlfriend again before I come out.'

Polly gasped and swung round, to see his laughing eyes teasing her. Snatching the phone, she held it to her ear and heard the dialling tone. 'Rat!' she laughed, and hung it up again. 'Matt, you were joking, weren't you?'

He grinned and nodded. 'This time! I want a quick shower and something to eat before I go out—and the next time I make love to you, it's going to take a damn sight longer than half an hour!'

It was nearly midnight by the time he came back. They had eaten the casserole together, Matt dressed again, Polly in his towelling robe with the sleeves rolled up countless times and the belt pulled tight. After he left, she cleared the kitchen up and sat watching television until nearly eleven-thirty, then went up to bed to wait for him there.

He let himself in and found her note, then after letting the dog out and locking up, he ran lightly upstairs and came to a halt in the bedroom doorway.

She was lying asleep, her hair tousled, a soft smile on her lips, and the quilt was twisted round her waist.

Matt stripped off his clothes and eased into bed beside her.

With a tiny, satisfied little sound, she snuggled up against him and relaxed, like a boneless cat. Matt curled himself around her with a lazy smile and fell asleep.

The phone rang again at three-thirty, and again at five, shortly after he got back.

He didn't get in again until nearly eight, and by this time he had had enough. He was grey with exhaustion, and Polly knew that he had lost the patient in the middle of the night.

Torn between staying to comfort him and letting

him sleep, Polly slipped out of bed, pulled on her
clothes and left him a note. Then she took the phone
off the hook, let Taffy out for a run and went to the
surgery, letting herself in and changing the tape on
the answer-phone. From that moment on, it would
call Dr Haynes. Leaving the cell-phone on its hook,
she went home to bed.

Bear was sitting on the pillow, and with a smile
she lifted him up and put him on the dressing-table.
'That's it, old fellow! Thanks for all the years of
loyal service.' She gave him a fond pat and snuggled
into the bed, her eyes drifting shut on the memories
of yesterday.

Matt surfaced at twelve and rang to thank her for
bailing him out. He was driving down to London to
spend the rest of the day with his parents, and asked
Polly if she could take Taffy out for a run and feed
him that evening.

A part of her was hurt that he didn't ask her to go
with him, but she had patients to visit for routine
dressing changes and wouldn't have had time
anyway. She didn't see him again until Friday, and
by this time she was missing him dreadfully. She also
had a cold, and with a commiserating cuddle he sent
her home to bed at the end of the day.

He popped in during the course of the evening to
bring her a drink and some aspirin, and then left her
to sleep. He was on call over the weekend, and it
was Monday evening before they could get away
together.

By this time reality had caught up with Polly, and
she waited until they had cleared away after their

meal and were sitting together in the sitting-room to broach the subject that was troubling her.

In fact Matt introduced it quite naturally by pulling her into his arms and kissing her lingeringly.

'How do you feel about an early night?' he asked, a sensuous smile about his lips.

Polly took a deep breath. 'I'm glad you mentioned that. Matt, the other night—did you do anything about birth control?'

'What?' He froze, and the look of shock on his face answered Polly's question.

'Oh, damn,' she said quietly. 'I was afraid of that.'

'Hell, Polly, you must know I didn't—why didn't you say something?'

She gave a short, bitter laugh. 'Why me? I was in no state to think of anything except what you were doing to me. I frankly wouldn't have noticed if you'd come to bed in a party hat and streamers. Why not you? Why didn't you think of it?'

'I did—but you're on the Pill, surely? I didn't think it was necessary——'

'Why should I be on the Pill?'

Matt stared at her in amazement. 'Perhaps because you knew this was going to happen?'

She shook her head numbly. 'It wasn't meant to. I really—oh, God.'

'Well, why did you have those pills?'

'What pills?'

Matt sighed and ran his hand through his hair in exasperation. 'At the party—Rebecca knocked your handbag off the table, and everything fell out—including your pills.'

A sick feeling crawled through Polly. 'I meant to explain—they were Rebecca's.'

'What on earth were they doing in your bag?'

'It wasn't my bag, it was hers. When you picked up the pills I saw the look on her face, and——'

'You jumped in and rescued her. Oh, my God! Polly, why didn't you explain to me? You must have known what I would think!'

'I—I forgot. That evening—you told me all about Elaine—I just forgot the whole incident.'

'How convenient.' His voice was bitter.

Polly was shocked. She could feel everything slipping away from her, but she didn't know what to do and everything she said seemed to make it worse.

'What do you mean, convenient? Anybody would think I had staged the whole thing to mislead you!'

He gave a short laugh. 'Oh, no, Polly, you're too naïve for that, but I wouldn't put it past you to take advantage of it if it helped your case!'

'Matt, I don't know what you're talking about——'

He stood up and paced away from her, turning in front of the fire and standing glaring at her, hands on hips. He was blocking the heat from the fire—that must be why cold fingers of dread were inching ever tighter round her heart.

'This whole seduction scene—bringing round the Christmas tree, the lunch, the presents, the rose on the pillow—all of it designed to seduce me with sentimental clap-trap——' His voice was rising, his face flushed with anger, and Polly watched in horror as he waved his hand around the room that she had decorated with such love. 'I told you I didn't want it, but you wouldn't damn well listen—perhaps you'll believe me now!'

He seized the little tree and hurled it across the room. The wire tore free, cutting out the fairy-lights, and in the sudden draught cards fluttered and fell to the floor.

Then he whirled round and left the room and she heard him in the bedroom upstairs, opening and shutting drawers. She sat numbly, staring at the doorway, until he reappeared.

He was deadly calm now, dressed in a track suit and trainers, looking strangely expressionless.

'When is your next period due?' he asked abruptly.

'Next week,' she whispered.

'Bingo.' He swore.

'Matt, we could make it work——'

'Make what work?'

'Us—together—we could work it out. It's not as if we don't love each other——'

'What makes you think I love you?' he asked, his voice incredulous.

'You told me—you said so——'

'When?'

Polly swallowed the lump in her throat. 'When you—when we made love.'

His face twisted with what looked like pain, but the expression was banished so fast Polly thought she must have imagined it.

'People say all sorts of things under those conditions,' he said flatly. 'You don't want to take it too seriously.'

Polly closed her eyes. So he was denying it. But

he surely couldn't have made love to her the way he had if he didn't love her?

'Matt, you must have meant it! The way you made love to me——'

He laughed coldly. 'It's called technique, sweetheart. Anyone can do it.'

'So you just screwed me for kicks, then?' Her voice was calm, with only a slight tremor.

'That's right.'

There was a tremor in his voice, too, but Polly didn't hear it, only the words.

'Well, I'm sorry if I misread it, but under the circumstances I think I could be forgiven the mistake. . .'

'Polly——' His face was anguished, the pain no longer disguised. 'How could you do this to us?'

'Me?' she screamed, her control gone. 'It takes two to tango, Dr Gregory—or didn't your medical training cover that? If you were so hysterically hell bent on not causing a pregnancy, wouldn't it have been prudent to check that I *was* on the Pill before you made love—sorry, *screwed* me?'

'I didn't think—it was the last thing on my mind——'

'Exactly! So it's *our* fault, and if I'm pregnant it will be *our* baby.'

The silence vibrated between them, charged with unbearable emotion. Finally, unable to stand it any longer, Matt broke it.

'Just remember this—if you're pregnant, you're on your own. I won't marry you. You won't get a damn thing from me. I've travelled that road before, and never again. It's not a good enough reason.'

Stepping into the room, he lifted the key from the beam over the fire and handed it to Polly. 'Here. You'd better keep this. I have no use for it.'

Then turning on his heel, he left, closing the door quietly behind him.

Polly gave him a minute to get away from the cottage before gathering up her few things and heading for the door.

She left the front door key on the dresser in the hall, patted Taffy and let herself out.

There was a fine drizzle misting over everything— at least, that was the excuse she gave for not being able to see. Climbing into her car, she started it up and reversed out into the lane, turning automatically towards her cottage. She didn't glance in the rear-view mirror, or she would have seen Matt standing in the lane, staring after her, a look of absolute desolation on his face.

She let herself into her cottage. The fire had gone out and it was cold in the way it hadn't been for ages. She didn't bother to light it, but climbed the stairs slowly and went into her bedroom.

'Sorry, Bear,' she said, and picked him up, hugging him to her chest.

Then the tears came, hot and heavy, with great racking sobs that tore her throat and made her head ache.

Hours later she got up stiffly and made herself a drink, took some aspirin and filled a hot water bottle. She wished she had some sleeping pills, but with the possibility of a new life inside her she wouldn't have taken them even if she'd had them.

Instead she lay and considered the options open

to her. Whatever the outcome, of course, she would have to leave the practice, but until she knew about the baby she wouldn't be able to make any other plans.

She wondered how she would feel if she did have a child. Lots of women managed to raise a child on their own, and if she couldn't have Matt, then maybe she could at least have his child.

Her grandmother used to tell her to be careful what you wished for, because you might just get it.

Polly squeezed her eyes shut tight, her lips moving in a silent prayer.

'Please give me his child,' she whispered, over and over, until sleep claimed her.

She dreamed of a dark-haired boy, with eyes the colour of granite under clear water, and a haunting smile that made the tears slip down her cheeks.

She woke with a wet pillow and a heavy weight on her heart. In the cold light of day, wishing for his child seemed a foolish thing to do, but she comforted herself with the knowledge that it had been too late for fate to intervene—either she was pregnant, or she wasn't. Only time would tell.

In the days that followed, Matt avoided her except for absolutely necessary professional contact—which meant the whole of the following Monday afternoon, of course.

He looked awful—tired and crabby, as if he hadn't slept. Jane Reed came in for her post-natal check up and seemed well and happy. Polly was pleased that things were working out well for them—after all, just because her life was a mess. . .

Mrs Major, too, was settling down to the idea of pregnancy, and Ms Harding had been confirmed as expecting twins.

Having had time to get used to the idea, she was pleased. 'Saves having to go through pregnancy twice, and I expect we might have wanted another one!' she said with a laugh.

Then it was New Year's Eve. Polly spent it alone, wondering what the year would hold for her. As the days went by, she grew more and more sure of the answer.

All around her everyone was blooming. Mrs Reed was coping beautifully in her new house, and the children had settled down remarkably quickly.

Even Mrs Robinson seemed to be getting on well. She came back on Thursday, a week into the new year, to see Matt to have her IUCD checked, and Polly chaperoned while Matt examined her.

'Looks fine,' he confirmed, and she smiled, slightly embarrassed.

'Good. I thought I'd better check. Don't want any accidents at this stage in the proceedings!'

Matt's face twisted. 'Quite,' he said with a slightly bitter smile. 'You should be perfectly safe. Have you had any more thoughts about reconstructive surgery?'

'Maybe later,' she said. 'There are more important things to think about for now.'

'They must be getting on better,' Polly said after she had left. 'I'm so glad.'

He sighed and ran his hand through his hair. 'Lucky them.' He glanced at Polly, and then looked away again. 'Any news?'

She didn't pretend not to know what he was talking about.

'No. No news. I'm three days overdue.'

The silence would have stretched on indefinitely if the phone hadn't rung. It was Mike Haynes.

'He wants to see you in his office,' Matt told her, and she grabbed the excuse and left.

'I want to talk to you about your resignation,' Mike said.

Polly sighed. 'Mike, there really is nothing more I can say. I'm sorry to let you down——'

'Polly, why?'

She swallowed. 'Personal reasons.'

'Matt?' She nodded reluctantly, and he sighed. 'You seemed to be getting on so well—are you sure it's such a serious problem that you can't work round it?'

Polly looked candidly at him. 'I think I'm pregnant. He doesn't want to know. . .' Her face crumpled, and she dropped it into her hands and wept.

'Oh, my poor dear girl—there, there, you get it out of your system.'

He laid a comforting hand on her arm, and Polly stifled the urge to giggle hysterically. If only she could—but it took a bit more than a few tears to get a baby out of one's system, and she wasn't sure she wanted to, anyway.

Pulling herself together with an effort, she blew her nose and looked out of the window. It was raining again—it always seemed to be raining these days.

'Mike, please don't tell anyone about the baby—

it would be easier for all of us, I think—anyway, I'm not even sure yet.'

'Take care. I imagine you'll keep it.'

Polly's head shot up. 'Of course! It's Matt's baby. . .'

Mike's mouth tightened in anger.

'I've got a good mind to have a serious talk with that young man.'

'No!' Polly was appalled. 'No, Mike, you mustn't! Promise me!'

After a second or two, he let his breath out on a ragged sigh. 'You're probably right. I doubt it would do any good. He's got such a hell of a chip on his shoulder after the job Elaine did on him—if there's anything I can do to help, just ask, Polly. And of course I won't say anything if you don't want me to. Anyway,' he frowned, 'I thought you were on the Pill?'

Polly could have laughed out loud. 'Yes, well, we all make mistakes,' she mumbled, and left him with that ambiguous comment.

By the following Monday she was sure—sure, and sick.

Matt stuck his head round her door at the end of morning surgery. 'Got an abscess here that needs draining and packing—would you assist, please?'

Nodding, she followed him into the little theatre. She had prepared it earlier for the usual minor surgical emergencies that often cropped up during the course of the day, and it was ready to go.

While Matt gave the man the local anaesthetic, Polly laid out the necessary surgical implements,

dressings and so forth. She tried not to look at the
swollen and angry lump on the man's forearm,
caused by neglecting a small puncture wound from
barbed wire.

While the anaesthetic took effect, Matt scrubbed
up and Polly tied the gown for him, every brush of
her fingers like an electric shock. The heat of his
body through the fine cotton of his shirt seemed to
scorch her, and she just wanted to lay her head
against his back and wrap her arms around his waist
and weep.

Instead she took up her station by the patient,
joking with him to ease his nerves.

Matt joined her, and she was acutely conscious of
his body so close to hers. So, apparently, was he.

'Could you give me a little elbow room, please,
Nurse Barnes?' he asked almost curtly. Polly
stepped sharply out of his way.

He picked up the scalpel and stroked it across the
skin, and immediately there was a great gush of
putrid matter from the abscess.

'Swab, please,' he murmured.

Polly picked up the forceps, opened them to lift a
swab and felt a rush of nausea.

'I'm—I'm sorry!' she gasped, and ran from the
room, reaching the sink in her room just in time.
She stayed like that, bent over the sink with her
head resting on the cool metal of the tap, for several
minutes while the nausea rolled around and gradually retreated.

Then she washed her face and hands in cold water
and straightened up slowly, looking at herself in the

mirror. Matt was standing behind her, his face pale and set. Their eyes locked.

'I'm sorry,' she said quietly. 'I'm all right now. Do you want me to come back?'

'No, I've finished.' He closed his eyes. 'It's definite, isn't it? You've got the look. I'm sorry, Polly. I warned you I couldn't be what you wanted. Will you be all right?'

'Why should you care?' she snapped.

'Of course I care!' he said harshly.

'Of course you do—you've just got a funny way of showing it! Don't worry, Matt,' she said, suddenly weary of the whole conversation. 'I'll be fine. Just leave me alone, please.'

He opened his mouth to say something, then changed his mind and closed it. Without another word, he turned on his heel and left, his face grim.

Polly sagged against the desk, her head in her hands, and wished she didn't have to work her notice. It was going to be the longest month of her life.

CHAPTER TEN

As years went, it hadn't got off to a very auspicious start, Polly thought wearily. She lay in bed, staring at the ceiling and stalling until the last possible minute before forcing herself out of bed.

Being upright meant being sick, she was fast discovering, and all the folklore in the world wasn't going to change that. She tried nibbling constantly, fasting, taking an apple and cold water to bed at night so she could eat and drink them before rising—the only thing she couldn't try, of course, was getting her husband to bring her a cup of tea—Matt having voted himself out of the role.

It didn't matter, though. She was sure tea wouldn't have worked either. In fact, the very thought had her feet hitting the floor in a mad dash to the bathroom.

The only consolation, she told herself some time later, was that it was of necessity a self-limiting condition.

Fighting down waves of nausea, she dressed slowly in her dark blue uniform, and noticed absently that the top was beginning to pull tight. Just another hiccup in the system, she thought, and finished dressing halfheartedly. Her uniform wouldn't have to last her long, after all.

Another Monday, she thought—the last one before she left. Tomorrow she was seven weeks pregnant—nearly five weeks since she and Matt had been blissfully, deliriously happy—so happy that they hadn't had the sense to think.

Now she was so miserable she couldn't think, but the prospect of the end of the week filled her with dread.

They hadn't found a replacement yet, but were interviewing this week. Mike had asked Polly to stay on until they found someone, but she had refused, explaining that she felt so ill she was hardly able to work.

In fact it was little to do with morning sickness, which so far had worn off about mid-morning and only returned at the end of the day, and far more to do with the fact that Matt was barely civil to her when they had to work together, and avoided her on all other possible occasions.

Sighing wearily, Polly buttoned her coat and made her way out to the car. There had been a frost again that night, and she had to do battle with the ice coating her windscreen before she could see to drive.

The roads were probably like glass, she thought, and emerged cautiously from her drive, peering to left and right. She was about to pull out when a car came round the corner from her right like a bat out of hell and slid on the ice, gliding gracefully into her off-side front wing with a tinkling crash. Her car bounced backwards and came to a gentle halt.

A young man got out, shook his head in dismay and approached her.

'Er, sorry, I seem to have hit you,' he said lamely.

'You do, don't you?' Polly said drily, climbing out to assess the damage. She was surprised at how unmoved she was by the whole incident. Must be the bovine hormones, she thought with a chuckle.

The young man shot her a funny look. 'Are you all right?' he asked worriedly.

She laughed aloud. 'Yes, I'm fine. How about you?'

'I'm OK, but your car's a bit crocked up, We'd better swap details, I suppose.'

That done, and the damage found to be largely cosmetic, he went on his way and Polly tried again.

This time she made it to the surgery without incident, and was soon headlong into the routine. Ear syringing, inoculations, dressing—and of course Mr Grey, whose ulcer was finally almost healed.

'How's the great romance going, Polly my dear?' he asked with a twinkle.

'There is no romance, Mr Grey,' she told him, and something in her tone must have alerted him.

'Then he's more foolish than I gave him credit for,' he retorted. 'A blind man on a galloping horse could see how things were between you—ah, well, lass, don't worry. Plenty more fish in the sea.'

'Not for me, Mr Grey,' she said quietly, and after that he fell silent, shocked by the sad resignation in her voice.

The day dragged. Matt was terse and uncommunicative during the ante-natal clinic, and Polly left as soon as she could after surgery, conscious that her time with him was severely limited and yet unable to endure another minute in his company.

It had been a bitch of a day, Matt thought morosely. Polly seemed to be everywhere, smiling and laughing at everyone but him. It was a front; he knew that, just as he knew why she was doing it.

She was doing it for the same reason he was—because that was the only way to preserve her sanity. Pretend that nothing's wrong, and perhaps all the bogey-men will go away.

It used to work when I was a boy, he thought. Why not now?

Because then the bogey-men weren't real, whereas now—now they were all of his own making.

Damn, why did this have to happen?

He drove home, took the dog out and was just coming back when he bumped into Mr Grey.

'I want a word with you, young man!' he said, stopping in front of Matt so that he couldn't get past without being rude.

'What can I do for you, Mr Grey?' he asked.

'Do? You can stop breaking that poor young Polly's heart, for a start. She's a good woman, and she thinks the world of you. I would have thought you'd have had more sense than to let her go. You'll never find another one like her, mark my words. One in a million, and yet you're too blind or too stupid to see it.'

'Mr Grey, I really don't think——'

'I know, son, none of my business. Well, when it comes to medicine, I grant you you know more than I do. But when it comes to love, experience counts for a lot. Polly reminds me of my Martha—good, true, honest as the day is long. Don't let her slip through your fingers, lad. She's too much of a prize.'

Matt closed his eyes and swallowed hard.

'It's too late, Mr Grey.'

'No. It's never too late, son. You go and have a chat with her. She won't turn you away.'

With that he stepped round Matt and continued down the pavement. Matt stayed where he was until Taffy's anxious whining brought him back to the present, then he pulled himself together and almost ran back into the house.

Changing quickly, he jumped into the car and headed off towards Polly's house.

As he reached the outskirts of town, he saw a flashing blue light bouncing off the trees in the distance; as he approached, he realised there was more than one set, then he rounded the corner and braked to a halt. In front of him were several vehicles, and tyre-marks all over the road. The cars involved in the collision had been moved to one side and police were there sweeping up glass. Matt frowned. There was an ambulance there still, and with a sinking heart he pulled over behind it and went to assist. He hoped it wouldn't take long—for once his professional zeal had deserted him and he only wanted to get to Polly.

The ambulance crew were just freeing a man from the wreckage of his van. He didn't appear to be injured, merely shaken. Matt approached them, identified himself and asked if he was needed in any way.

'Don't think so, Doc. We got the worst one away in the first ambulance. Hell of a mess.'

Matt lifted his head and surveyed the wrecked cars. Suddenly his heart began to pound and there was a roaring in his ears.

'The driver of that Fiesta—where is she?' he

asked, and he found himself holding his breath for the reply.

'The little nurse? Gone in the first wagon, Doc.'

'Where did they go?' he asked, his lips suddenly dry.

'Audley. A & E.'

'Do you need me?' he asked, fervently hoping he would say no.

The bemused man shook his head. 'No. Hey, there's no rush, mate,' the man called after him.

Matt ran back to his car, gunned the engine and shot off back the way he had come.

Whatever did he mean, no rush? Dear God, no— not that! Heart racing, adrenalin surging, he completed the twenty-minute journey in less than fifteen minutes, slewing to a halt outside the A & E department.

He ran through the double doors, catching his shoulder on one as it opened too slowly for him, then he ran down the corridor and through the doors that said 'Staff Only'.

A burly man in a white coat was walking down the corridor towards him, and Matt grabbed him by the arm.

'Where is she? Polly—Polly Barnes? She came in some time ago in an ambulance—there was an accident in Longridge—I need to see her. Is she——?'

He freed his arm gently and placed a hand on Matt's shoulders. 'Calm down, old chap. Start again. Who is it you're looking for?'

Matt paused and forced himself to draw a deep

breath. 'She's small—dark hair, curly—her name's Polly Barnes. She was brought in——'

'Yes, yes, you said all that. Hang on, let's see if we can get some help. Who are you, exactly?'

'Gregory—Matthew Gregory. I'm in general practice in Longridge——'

'Ah, Mike Haynes' new chap. Nice to meet you. I'm Jim Harris. Look, there's Dr Henderson—we'll see if she can shed any light on your Polly. Bron! Give me a hand, could you? We're trying to track down a Polly Barnes, but I can't see her on the board. What cubicle's she in?'

'The last time I saw her she was in Crash with a cardiac arrest. I don't know what happened to her after that. I was with the neurology reg.'

Matt closed his eyes, despair washing over him. All he could see was Polly's car, the wing crushed like an eggshell. God knows how she had been flung around inside it. Cardiac arrest. Please, God, don't let it be too late!

'Are you all right?'

Matt leant against the wall and waited for his head to clear. The shock was taking its toll, and he could hardly stand. He nodded at the doctor standing beside him, her clear grey eyes troubled.

'Come and get a cup of tea, and I'll see if I can find out where they've taken her.' She led him towards a door that said 'Staff Room', and pushed the door open.

A tall, fair-haired man was standing in the middle of the room, laughing at something one of the other doctors had said. He looked up as they went in, and Matt stared at him. A feeling of sick dread stole over

him, a sort of déjà vu run mad. Oliver
Henderson, registrar and friend during a part of his
life he would give anything to forget—the man who
had supported him through the agony of his marriage
and subsequent loss—here, like the angel of death,
he thought, cropping up whenever tragedy struck.

'What are you doing here, Oliver?' he asked
hoarsely.

The man frowned slightly in puzzlement. 'Matt?
Matthew Gregory?'

But Matt suddenly lost interest in his old friend,
because someone in a dark blue sister's uniform had
stood up and was walking towards him. She was
thin, much thinner than he had realised, and there
were dark circles under her eyes that stood out
against her pale face, but she was unmistakably,
definitely alive.

'Ah, there you are, we were looking for you,'
Bron said, but he didn't hear.

There was a roaring in his ears, and he swayed on
his feet. His voice was out of his control. He tried to
say her name, but all that would come out was a
harsh whisper. It was a vision. He was dreaming—
or his eyes needed testing. He squeezed them
shut. . .

Polly's eyes widened. Matt was standing there trans-
fixed, swaying on his feet, all the colour drained
from his face. As she watched, he tried to say her
name, and then his eyes closed.

'Matt?' she said. 'Matt, whatever is the matter?
You look as if you've seen a ghost!'

'Polly?' His voice was incredulous. His eyes

opened again, and gradually his colour returned. 'Are you all right?'

'Of course I'm all right—why shouldn't I be?'

'I thought you were—Dr Henderson said—oh, God. I thought. . .'

Polly returned his feverish gaze with a level stare, unable to allow herself to trust the blaze of feeling on his face.

'I'm fine. I arrived just after the accident happened, and got myself involved, like a fool. This man arrested and I came along for the ride, to give them a hand, because they were busy with the head injuries chap.'

He let out his breath in a long, shaky sigh.

'But your car—what about your dented wing?'

She shook her head. 'That happened this morning, nothing to do with this acident. Some bloke skidded on the ice. It was nothing——'

'Nothing? Damn it, if you'd been hurt——'

'Well, I wasn't!' she snapped, her patience at an end. Why this sudden concern for her welfare— unless. . .? Her heart contracted with pain. 'You don't have to worry, Matthew, your precious baby's fine.'

There was a shocked gasp from the man beside her, but Polly ignored him. Dashing the tears from her eyes, she hunted for her coat and bag, and then looked up at Bron. 'Is there somewhere round here I can get a taxi?'

'I'll take you,' Matt said, but she snatched her arm away from him.

'Leave me alone. I don't want to go with you.'

'Polly, please, I need to talk to you.'

She turned to him, eyes blazing. 'There is nothing you could have to say that I could possibly want to hear!'

Matt paused, his throat working. Did she dare believe he really was concerned about her, or was it just his baby? She didn't know, couldn't think clearly enough to work it out. She nearly relented, but she was at the end of her tether and she just wanted to go somewhere quiet and lie down. She closed her eyes against the light.

'Polly, please listen!'

'Don't nag me, Matt. I don't want to know. You've ignored me for weeks—why get so het-up now?'

'Because I thought you were dead! Damn it, Polly, I came looking for you to ask you to marry me, and I found this accident, your car there with its wing smashed to a pulp, and then someone tells me you're in Crash with a cardiac arrest—what the hell am I supposed to think?'

Polly stared at him, unable to believe her ears. He had come to ask her to marry him? Why?

'Why?' she said, her voice bitter.

'Why what?'

'Why ask me to marry you? Or more precisely, who? Me, or the mother of your child?'

Matt gave an exasperated shrug. 'But you *are* the mother of my child.'

'No.' Polly shook her head firmly. 'I'm the mother of *my* child. You said at the time that you wanted nothing to do with it. Why the sudden change of heart, Matt?'

He stared at the floor for a long while, then looked

up, his eyes mirroring his confusion. 'I don't understand. I thought you wanted us to get married.'

'I did—I do. But only for the right reasons. I once
told you I'd take whatever you could give me, but
I've changed my mind. I'm not that strong, Matt. I
want it all, or none of it. I don't want to be just the
mother of your child.'

'What the hell is the difference?' he demanded.

Polly shook her head in despair. 'You really don't
see it, do you?' Her eyes squeezed shut, but a tear
slid past her lashes and tracked slowly down her
cheek.

'Polly. . .' Matt's voice was agonised, but she
steeled herself and turned away.

'Goodbye, Matt.'

'Polly, wait!'

But she turned away, her heart aching with the
weight of unshed tears, and headed instinctively
towards the exit.

'Go after her.' The voice was calm, authoritative,
and familiar.

'It's too late, Oliver. She doesn't want to know—
and it's probably just as well. It would be a disas-
ter——'

'Rubbish. Why should it?'

'It's the same thing all over again, and I can't
stand it. Damn it, she's pregnant!' he groaned, but
Oliver grabbed him by the sleeve and jerked him
upright.

'So what? It happens to the best of us. Does that
give you the right to punish her for what Elaine did
to you?'

Matt's eyes widened, and he shook his head in denial.

'Is she like Elaine?'

The silence stretched out endlessly, then he shook his head again, more firmly. 'No,' he said quietly, 'she's nothing like Elaine.'

'Then go after, Matt. Tell her you love her. Please?'

For the second time in an hour, Matt found himself on the receiving end of the same advice.

'What the hell,' he muttered, 'you can't all be wrong,' and headed for the door.

Polly was finding it very hard to stand up. A broken heart and pregnancy sickness made rotten bedfellows, she realised, and clamped down another wave of nausea.

'Can you tell me where I can get a taxi?' she asked the receptionist, but before the woman could answer, a firm, warm arm came steadyingly around her waist.

'I'll take you home.'

'Matt, I——'

'Please?'

Polly felt a tear slip down her cheek, but she couldn't be bothered to do anything about it. Another one joined it. 'Don't bully me, Matt,' she whispered brokenly. 'I really can't take it.'

His jaw clenched, but his arms around her were gentle.

'I won't say a word. Come on, let's get you out of here.'

She went with him, as much as anything because

she could no longer fight back. She could feel the
hard jut of his hip as they walked, and the warm
solidity of his body protectively against her side.
Surrendering her last shred of self-control, she
allowed herself to sag against him, and his arm
tightened, drawing her more firmly into his side.

'Nearly there,' he murmured, and helped her into
the car.

Halfway back, in the silence he had promised,
Polly felt the roiling nausea again.

'Matt, stop!' she moaned, and half-leapt, half-fell
out of the car. Within seconds he was beside her,
smoothing her hair back from her brow, holding her
firmly against him until she felt better. Then he
helped her back into the car and wrapped a rug
around her knees.

'I'll be hot——'

'No, you won't, because you'll have the window
open. All right now?'

Polly closed her eyes and nodded. She couldn't
bear to look at him—his concern, his solicitous
attitude—but who for? Her, or his child? At the
moment they went together, but later—how would
he be then? She snuggled down in the rug and tried
not to think.

She didn't open her eyes until the car drew to a
halt.

'This is your house,' she said blankly.

Matt opened her door and lifted the rug away,
releasing her seatbelt and helping her out of the car.

She resisted. 'This is your house,' she repeated,
more firmly.

'Yes. I told you I was taking you home.'

'Matt, I——'

'Come on, darling. Inside, up to bed and get some sleep. You're white as a sheet. We'll talk about it later.'

She allowed him to lead her upstairs to his bedroom, take off her coat and dress and push her gently down into the bed, covering her with the soft downy quilt. The bed smelt wonderful—fresh, clean, but with just the faintest tang of Matt clinging to it. Polly stopped fighting and snuggled down into the covers, asleep almost instantly.

She woke hours later, feeling much better and starving hungry. She lay for a while staring at the ceiling and regretting the fact that by the time she had found something to eat she wouldn't be able to keep it down, and then she took a deep breath and threw off the quilt.

'Hi. . .'

She froze. 'Matt.'

There was a strained laugh. 'Who else? Are you feelling better?'

'Mmm. Starving—thirsty, really. I don't know what I want.'

Apart from a cuddle, but she dared not ask—at least until she knew what was going on.

'Stay there, I'll get you something.'

Polly sagged back against the pillows, her lip caught between her teeth. If only she could be sure he wanted her for herself. . .

'Try this.' His voice was soft, close to her. She opened her eyes.

He was holding a tray with a little bowl of rice, and a glass of something pale and cloudy.

'Pressed apple juice. Just sip it. And I brought you some boiled rice with lots of salt—Mrs Major's idea. She mentioned it the other day. Try it.'

He hovered over her while she sipped the juice.

'It's lovely, thanks.'

He perched on the bed and coaxed her to eat, and then when she had had enough he took the tray.

'I'll leave you alone now,' he murmured, turning the light down. 'Try and get some more sleep.'

She didn't find her voice until he was almost at the door, then she only managed a croak.

'What's the matter?'

She hesitated. Could she say, Come back here and tell me you love me—me, not your child. Did she dare? What if he couldn't say it? Oh, what could she say?

'Thank you, Matt.'

'You're welcome.'

She couldn't see his face with the landing light behind him, but she thought she saw his shoulders droop—with disappointment? Had he hoped she would say more? How could she? She was waiting for him to make a move—but not yet. Not while she was so tired.

She slid down the bed and closed her eyes, and sleep claimed her almost instantly.

She woke later needing the bathroom, and Matt was there to make sure she had everything she needed; she discovered her nightdress and wash things, so he must have been over to her cottage. His thoughfulness brought a lump to her throat.

She took off her clothes, showered quickly and brushed her teeth, and then made her way back to his bedroom. He was waiting, sitting on the edge of his bed in that revealing towelling robe that showed his legs off to such unfair advantage.

She looked quickly away.

'Thank you for getting my things,' she said in a small voice.

'You're welcome, Is there anything else you need for the night?'

She shook her head. Only you, she thought, but he left her alone again with her thoughts. When is he going to say something? she wondered.

She woke in the night to a sensation of warmth and solid comfort. Matt was beside her, his face against her hair, his chest warm and hard beneath her hand. Her head was cradled on his shoulder, and under her ear she could hear the steady, reassuring thud of his heart.

'Polly?' His voice was a whisper, a mere breath of sound in the quiet night.

'Yes,' she murmured, and eased closer.

Their legs tangled, and Matt caught his breath.

'Hold me,' she pleaded, and he groaned.

'I am holding you.'

'No, tighter. Closer. I've missed you so much——'

Her voice broke, and she turned her face into his chest, her arms going round him and clinging hard, as if she could imprint herself on him so he would realise that he loved her.

'I've missed you, too. Marry me, Polly,' he murmured against her hair.

'Matt, I can't.' She lifted her head away, seeking his eyes in the almost-dark.

'Why? I can't stand it any longer. I wasn't going to say or do anything. I was going to let you go, have the baby, tell me or not—but I can't. I need you here, with me. Say yes. Don't go—don't leave me.' His voice was unsteady, vulnerable. Polly's heart quickened, then slowed again as common sense reared its head.

'Matt, I can't. What if you wake up one morning and realise that it's all a dreadful mistake? I couldn't bear to feel I'd trapped you the way Elaine did. I can't make you unhappy for the rest of your life.'

'But you will do, Polly, if you walk away. I can't distinguish between you and the mother of my child. You *are* the mother of my child—and I wouldn't have it any other way. But last night I didn't even give the baby a thought. All I could think about was you—I'd even forgotten you were pregnant until you said something about it. Polly, I love you——'

He broke off, his voice ragged and uneven, and in the dim light from the landing Polly could see his eyes bright with tears.

'You're still upset because you thought I'd died.'

'No! No! I'm just so afraid I've lost you. I've hurt you so badly—said so many awful things. The key——'

That hurt. To know you had no use for me——'

'I was lying—to you, and to myself. I can't live without you, Polly. Don't make me.'

Polly hesitated, afraid. Was he sure? Did he mean what he said? Could she trust him? He had rejected her once—could she bear it if he did it again? If not, then she really shouldn't give him the power. . .

'Wait. Stay here.'

His long legs swung out of the bed and he padded quietly across the floor and down the stairs, shrugging on his dressing-gown. She could hear him moving about in the sitting-room and the hall, and heard him murmuring to Taffy. Then he was coming back up, and across the bedroom.

The side of the bed dipped, and he switched on the bedside light.

'Here. I couldn't think of any other way to convince you.'

He tipped dozens of keys on to the quilt and then held them up one by one.

'This is the front door, the back door, the french door, the window locks, the radiator bleed screws, the car, the surgery, the garden shed, my suitcases, a trunk in the attic full of old papers and things, my desk, the piano, the deed box. . .'

Polly looked at him doubtfully, her heart in her throat. 'Haven't you forgotten one?'

He tried to smile, but his face crumpled and he looked away. Fishing in the pocket of his dressing gown, he brought out a heavy, rusty old key.

'It's not been used a lot, but you're welcome to it if you've any use for it.'

He held out his hand, palm up, with the key lying across it. Slowly, her heart filling with love, Polly reached out and took it.

'Does it work on your chastity belt?' she asked teasingly.

He eyed her searchingly. 'Is that a yes?'

She relented, and opened her arms. 'Yes. Yes, yes, yes, yes, yes!'

* * *

They were married on Friday afternoon, in a very simple ceremony at the little register office in Longridge, and went back to the Hayneses' house for a quiet reception. As well as the members of the practice and Matt's parents, there were only a small handful of guests including Bron and Oliver Henderson and their little daughter Livvy, and Mr and Mrs Grey. Polly was grateful to them for their interference, but she felt Matt would probably have come to his senses sooner or later. However, she was quite happy that it had been sooner!

Matt had explained that Oliver was the registrar at Guy's who had taken him under his wing after Elaine died. He had made a short and very funny speech at the reception, pickled with corny jokes about all their troubles being little ones, and doctors knowing better, all the while holding his squirming two-year-old daughter on one hip.

After the reception Matt and Polly headed back to the cottage, where Polly's few possessions from her rented cottage had been stacked in the spare bedroom awaiting her attention.

They were curled up in front of the fire sipping fruit juice and holding hands, deeply contented.

'My parents like you,' Matt murmured.

'Good. I liked them, too. Oliver's speech was very funny—were you really that useless as a houseman?' Polly asked

Matt chuckled. 'What did you think of him?'

'I liked him.'

'Mmm. Me too. I'm glad he's found such a super wife; he was a really good friend to me back then.

We must have them over to dinner when you can face food again.'

Polly smiled. 'I feel much better now. It must be to do with stress.'

Matt lifted her hand to his lips and kissed each finger in turn. 'No more stress. Quiet days and early nights——'

'You're insatiable,' Polly said with a chuckle.

'You complaining already?'

'No way.' she snuggled closer. Everything was perfect. Taffy was lying, his nose between his paws, inches from the woodburner, and on the beam above him was a row of keys—two in particular had been moved, and polished until they gleamed. They were hung side by side in the centre of the beam, linked with a gold ring that held them together. The ring had been soldered. As Matt said, there was no way they could accidentally drift apart.

Polly liked that idea.

Matt's hand laid gently on her tummy. 'I wonder what we're hatching?' he murmured.

'Do you mind?'

He shook his head. 'No. No, I don't mind at all so long as you're both well.' He lowered his head and kissed her. 'How about that early night, Pollyanna?'

She laughed, a little breathlessly because his lips were trailing slowly down her jaw and nibbling at her neck.

'This early?' she whispered.

His lips came to rest on the hollow of her throat, and her heart accelerated. Matt chuckled.

Oh, I think you're ready for bed, Pollyanna.'

She faked a yawn, and then shrieked with laughter

as he hoisted her up in his arms and headed for the stairs.

'Come on, Mrs Gregory. Your first lesson in wifely etiquette—no yawning on duty.'

'What if I do?' she asked lazily.

'You'll have to have even earlier nights.'

He dropped her gently on to the bed.

'Hardly seems worth getting up,' she offered mischievously.

'Mmm. What a good idea. . .'

The bed dipped beside her, and his mouth came down to claim hers—forever.

4 MEDICAL ROMANCES
AND 2 FREE GIFTS
From Mills & Boon

Capture all the excitement, intrigue and emotion of the busy medical world by accepting four FREE Medical Romances, plus a FREE cuddly teddy and special mystery gift. Then if you choose, go on to enjoy 4 more exciting Medical Romances every month! Send the coupon below at once to:

**MILLS & BOON READER SERVICE, FREEPOST
PO BOX 236, CROYDON, SURREY CR9 9EL.**

NO STAMP REQUIRED

YES! Please rush me my 4 Free Medical Romances and 2 Free Gifts! Please also reserve me a Reader Service Subscription. If I decide to subscribe, I can look forward to receiving 4 Medical Romances every month for just £6.40, delivered direct to my door. Post and packing is free, and there's a free Mills & Boon Newsletter. If I choose not to subscribe I shall write to you within 10 days - I can keep the books and gifts whatever I decide. I can cancel or suspend my subscription at any time. I am over 18.

EP19D

Name (Mr/Mrs/Ms)_____

Address_____

_____

_____ Postcode_____

Signature_____

— _MEDICAL_ ♥ ROMANCE —

The books for enjoyment this month are:

SAVING DR GREGORY Caroline Anderson
FOR LOVE'S SAKE ONLY Margaret Barker
THE WRONG DIAGNOSIS Drusilla Douglas
ENCOUNTER WITH A SURGEON Janet Ferguson

♥   ♥   ♥   ♥   ♥

Treats in store!

Watch next month for the following absorbing stories:

THE SINGAPORE AFFAIR Kathleen Farrell
CAROLINE'S CONQUEST Hazel Fisher
A PLACE OF REFUGE Margaret Holt
THAT SPECIAL JOY Betty Beaty